A Storm of Magic

Ashley Laino

EST.
2019
BLKDOG

A STORM
OF MAGIC

"She kissed me.
She kissed the devil.
Only a beautiful soul
Like her would kiss the
damned."

- Daniel Saint

CHAPTER ONE: MIRAH

All of my life there has been a darkness burning inside of me. It threatens to spill out and creep in the under groves and roots of the world until it envelops everything on the land, water, and air. The darkness is hungry, starving even, and there is no satiation. I was born a witch, but I fear that I may become a demon.

****

The jingle of the bells on the store door wake me from my mediations. I have found that I have been struggling to focus more and more, worries from my past have been resurfacing and all consuming, but our little pagan store did not get a lot of customers, so I was not going to let this one get away.

I grin broadly at a young couple perusing our crystal selection. The girl adjusts her dark rimmed glasses and smiles back at me, ruffling her pixie haircut. She tugs at the arm of her boyfriend whose hair was stacked into an impressively styled man bun. Hipsters. Thank god. They were our store's saving grace.

"Can I help you with anything," I call out politely.

"This store is fabulous!" The girl chimes back to me, "It has such a great aura, and I've been dying to try a good crystal cleanse. Finals have been a killer and my chakras are so misaligned."

My eyes start to water, I'm trying so hard not to roll my eyes at this girl's pretentious psychobabble. I can tell she doesn't know a word of what she's talking about, but thankfully, the occult has become trendy amongst college students, and they have been keeping our store afloat.

As I guide her through our crystal and gem collection, and explain the meaning and connotation of the different stones, I find myself starting to grow warm and beads of sweat started to form on my brow.

I eyed my customers to see if they were having any of the same reactions as me, but as I watched them examine a piece of rose quartz carefully, I knew that they were not having the same trouble I was.

The heat in face started to intensify and I found myself desperately wishing that they were gone. I take the stone that they wanted to purchase and make my way to the counter and watch them peak around the store. *These imposters have no respect.* A voice growled in my mind. I tried to ignore it, but I felt my face start to flush and the echoes in my mind started to roar. *Show them what real magic can do,* it whispered. *Cover them in warts, turn the trinkets in their hands to ash. Show them real power.*

My body was so hot I thought I might burst. I gripped my tingling hands on the edges of the counter and panted. My eyes began to roll back and I felt my energy spike to wild heights. I think the boyfriend asked me something, but with the roaring in my ear I couldn't hear him. The voice in my head had turned from murmurs to bellows, *Burn! Burn them where they stand.*

I feel my body start to sway and through the clouds of my vision, I can see the couple staring at me concerned. The hipster girl yells something to me that I can't hear, but I'm able to make out the word "Help" on her lips. I open my mouth to reassure her, warn her, cry out to her, but instead a guttural roar pours out of me and I feel all the heat in my body traveling to my fingertips as I start to convulse. I reach a hand towards the young pair and point a my index right between them. I stretch my mouth open even farther, so far that I can feel the corners of my mouth begin to ache. It feels like my mouth might tear, and just as I'm about to speak the spell that comes unbidden to my brain, I am suddenly whacked hard on the head and I fall gracelessly to the ground.

The blow, though painful, throws me back into my normal consciousness. When I'm able to raise myself from the ground, I rub my aching head and look around the store. Crystals have been thrown haphazardly around the floor and the hipster couple is gone. It seems that they made a break for it as soon as the opportunity was available.

I groan as I turn to the back of the store, where I see my Aunt Gerta, holding a stag encrusted chalice staring ahead at the front door. With a resigned sigh, she shakes her head and places the chalice back onto the store counter.

"Well, it looks like we shouldn't expect any positive reviews any time soon."

I apologize as I grip onto the nearest table and hoist myself up. I can feel an egg forming on the back of my head and it takes a minute to try a find my balance. Once I steady myself, a voice calls from the back of the store drawing both my aunt's and my attention.

"Enough of this Gerta. We've avoided this conversation for too long. Mirah needs help."

"She seems to be able to get up just fine. It was just a little love knock on the head." My Aunt Gerta calls back.

My aunt's partner Lila stands cross armed in the entrance way to the back room of the shop. Her short, grey hair is standing on end and her mouth is drawn into a sharp line of disapproval. I know that look. Lila has made a decision and there was no chance of getting her to back down.

"I'm not talking about the hit. She had a spike of power," My aunt Lila insists.

"She just starting to come into her power, and just needs some time and practice to control it. It's nothing some rest, study, and meditation can't fix." Gerta drawls trying to wave Lila away with a jeweled hand,

My aunt throws Lila one of her most charming smiles, but Lila doesn't budge an inch, expect for the small narrowing of her eyes.

"You know that's not true, Gerta. Stop trying to brush away what is happening to Mirah."

"What is happening to me?" I interject. This was not the first time I had felt my power overtake me in the past couple of months, but this was by far the most powerful possession I had experienced, and the most dangerous. For the first time in my life, I felt that I was actually starting to get scared of my magic.

Lila turns to me and her thin lips drop into an even deeper frown, "I don't know dear. That's what worries me. I've never seen anything like it and..." she turns and glares at my aunt, "a witch develops into her powers when she's thirteen. You were always a late bloomer Mirah, but at sixteen there is no way this you "coming into your powers.""

I look down at myself and almost chuckle. Late bloomer, was a serious understatement. Physically, at five feet tall, I was more of a never bloomer. Flat chested and petite, if I didn't watch what I wore, I could easily look like I was twelve years old. But, Lila was right. Even though I never grew much for my height, my powers have always been right on track if not ahead of my age. More importantly, whatever was happening, felt out of my control.

"Mirah," Lila begins, "Why don't you go inside and rest for a little bit. I need to talk to your aunt," I can tell be her tone that it's not a request. It's a command.

I made my way to the back of the store, to the door that connects our house to the store, but before I cross through the entranceway, I turn back and see my two aunts whispering fervently to one another. Any trace of humor from my aunt Greta's face has been erased and in place of a bemused smile, a tight line forms across her face making her seem older than her years.

Looking at my aunt's face makes my heart begin to sink. I know that if Gerta can't find the humor a situation, then it truly is serious. I look down at my hands, trying to read the lines in my palms so that I could understand what was happening to me. As I stared, I felt my hands start to tingle and I quickly clutch them into a fist to try a force the magic away.

However, the magic doesn't fade, rather it travels up my arms and through my body in static waves. I can feel the power from the top of my scalp to the bottom of my toes. I am fully charged and I feel electric. I am lighting that is going to crash, and crash soon.

CHAPTER TWO:

DARIEN

Purgatory is terribly boring. I mean I suppose that that's the point of it all, it's to force you to think about what you've done and how you can redeem yourself, but as I sit in this gray waiting room lost in time, I can help but wish there was at least a magazine I could flip through.

I look around me and take in the bare gray walls and a few sterile white chairs. There is are no doors or windows, so the whole area is deeply claustrophobic. Above me are gray tiles. There are one hundred and seventy-two tiles. I have had more than enough time to count every single one multiple times. The room is lit by a single, buzzing light that is impossible to turn off.

I sigh deeply and prop my feet on the chair besides me. I was seventeen when I died. I don't remember much about how it all ended for me. All I know is my last memory before the gray is a man screaming and a terrible cracking noise, like a firecracker followed by a bright light. I wonder if I was hit by a lightning bolt, that would be terribly exciting.

I stretch in discomfort and slink my back onto the floor, so that only my feet are resting on the chair. I can't help but wonder how old I would be now if I were still alive. There is no sense of time in this dull abyss. I could have been here for minutes or years. It was impossible to tell, and the only thing I'm able to do in this room is think.

These thoughts are interrupted by a screeching noise behind me. Startled, I roll over to my stomach and yelp as a I see a large tear in the blank space of the wall. The noise, like nails on a chalkboard, increases steadily and I have to clamp my hands over my ears. The rip grows larger, but all I can see within is a dark tunnel.

Crap. I guess the almighty have decided it's the dark world for me. Well at least it'll be a change of scenery.

As much as I try and joke, I can't stop my heart from racing at the fear of what new horror laid before me. Suddenly, the noise stopped, and the whole room was filled with an eerie silence. The wall had become a full tunnel and I wondered if I was supposed to make my way towards it, but before I could even move a finger, my question was answered for me.

It started at first as a loud dragging noise, followed by the sour and smoky smell of ash and body odor. My eyes widened, as a gnarled head of some deformed creature peeked through the tunnel opening and then slithered with a slop onto the floor.

I scrunch my nose, not just at the sight of this monster, but at its terrible smell as well. It must have been a person at some point, it still had some of the features. But time had turned it terribly twisted and rotten.

It had no legs, but rather used its spindly arms to drag itself to where it wanted to go. The spine was mangled into large knots and its flesh was covered in red, angry-looking boils. When it finally made its way out of the tunnel, it looked at me with red, round, bulging eyes. It's nose was pressed back so far into its head it all reminded me of some monstrous combination of a slug and a pug.

"Darien," It rasped.

"Present." I responded raising my hand. If I was going to be dragged into the bowels of hell, I at least want to have a little fun before I go.

"My master has a proposition for you," The creature grumbles on, apparently not amused by my antics.

"He will help you escape your purgatory, and give you life again, but it comes at a cost."

"What kind of cost?" I ask lazily, "If this… proposition involves me losing my sparkling good looks then I'll stay right here. I've always enjoyed my own company if I may say so myself."

The creature blinks at me, one eye at a time. It doesn't seem amused. That's unfortunate.

"My master's needs you to get someone to sign his book," The creature gargles out, drool dribbling down the side of its mouth.

"And your master is? Details, darling, details."

"My master is the king of darkness. My master is the lord of fire. My master is…"

"The Dark Warlock. Your master's the Dark Warlock. Got it," I prop my head on my heads intrigued, "Now that that's clear, what is this book and why on Earth does he need me, of all people to play librarian."

"He needs you to get the witch to sign his Book of Souls!" The monster spits out at me, "You have a set of skills that my master needs. You had some uses before you ended up here."

"What's in it for me. I don't exactly do favors for free."

"If you can get the witch to sign the book before the next full moon, you will be fully be brought back to life with all the riches you could ever dream, and when you die, you will have a place by the side of the King of Darkness himself," The cretin bellows at me, spittle flies from his gaping maw, "You will not suffer pain in the afterlife, but experience absolute power!"

"That sounds sweet, but what happens if I can't get this witch lady to sign your demon book?"

"Your life ends and your soul belongs to the darkness itself. There will be no glory for you, just pain."

I roll onto my back and stare at the bleak gray ceiling for a moment weighing my pros and cons. On one hand, I certainly didn't want to stay in purgatory any longer and it's not like I led a squeaky-clean life in the past. I certainly wasn't afraid to get my hands a bit dirty. But on the other hand, stealing and gambling was one thing, getting some stranger to sell their soul is entirely different, and the idea on ending up the Dark Warlock's lacky like this worm before me was not tempting.

"What if I don't agree to the deal at all?" I question.

"Then you remain here. Trapped as before." The answer rings through the bare walls with a note of finality. I took a moment and looked around the blank existence that I had been surviving through. There was nothing bad here. Nothing good either. It was simply living in nothing, and it was all terribly boring and if there was one thing that I hated more than anything else, it was being bored.

"Deal." I called to the monster nonchalantly. Let's get this party started.

There was a deafening silence, and for a second, I wondered if the creature hadn't heard me, but then a ear-piercing shriek rang out throughout the room. I turned and saw the monster squirming in agony, eyes bloodshot, and screaming. Its mouth was open so wide, I could see the blood and decay of its jowls. Finally, it clutched its deformed arms to its head and began to pull. It yelled and pulled and yelled and pulled, until the head split. The slug like appendages split. The whole demon was torn in half. As I inspected the carnage, I noticed a sleek black book had been trapped inside the creature.

I gently picked it up and noticed faint script along the spine of the book. Before I could take a closer look though, the writing disappeared. It didn't matter though. I knew that it was the Book of Souls, and before I could stop it, the book, itself, levitated and disappeared inside my chest, knocking the wind out of me, and making my veins burn.

The deal had been made. I needed to get the Dark Warlock his witch, or I would end up worse than dead.

I guess it's time to go on a witch hunt.

CHAPTER THREE:

MIRAH

As I waited for my aunts to return, I paced around our small, plush living room to kill some time, and to try and shake off my nerves.

Our house was not glamourous by any means, but it was every definition of the word "cozy." A large, red sofa, worn in the seats, stood proudly in the middle of the room across from an ornate, antique coffee table.

Beside the couch, was a sagging dark brown leather chair. It was claw tattered by all of the cats we've had over the years. The truth is, I have no idea how old that chair even is, we've had it as long as I can remember, but I do know that once you sit in it, you are bound to fall asleep in a matter of minutes if you're not careful. As a matter of fact, one of many of our small, black cats was snoozing peacefully on the seat.

There was no TV, my aunts were far too old-school for that, but against the wall were three large bookshelves. The shelves were lined with every form of text you could imagine: from books of philosophy to steamy romance novels that would make a sailor blush. Scattered amongst the shelves were a variety of knick-knacks and some family photos. Absentmindedly, I picked up a photo from when I was very small. I was on Greta's shoulders, apple picking, Lila was laughing and swinging a full woven basket.

I smiled at the memory and returned the picture to its place. There were lots of images of happy memories on these shelves, but there were no pictures of my mother or father.

In fact, I had no idea what either of my parents looked like. My mother died after childbirth, and I was given to my mother's sister Gerta to be raised. My aunts told me that I looked like my mother, but other than that, they almost never spoke of her.

As for my father, I knew even less. I was surrounded by women, which was great, but a part of me always longed for a father figure. Every time I tried to ask; my aunts would brusquely shove the question aside. He was not a good person was all they have ever told me. They were going to make sure I never ended up like him, they reassured me. As I grew older, I never asked more. I was happy with my aunts and saw them as my parents. I also didn't want to upset them. Now I wondered what kind of darkness laid in my gene pool.

My thoughts were interrupted when the door between our house and the store swung open. I turned to see both my aunts marching into the room quiet and unsmiling.

"Mirah, can you take a seat for a moment," Gerta remarked to me, motioning towards the couch.

I tentatively sat on the edge of the sofa, desperate to know what my aunts were going to say.

"Your aunt and I have been talking," Lila began. My Aunt Gerta's eyes were trained down to the floor.

"Your powers have begun to grow exponentially and your starting to develop skills that your aunt and I, frankly, cannot help you with. They are beyond our expertise."

"So, what does that mean for me," I ask nervously.

"Your aunt and I are just simple Hedge witches. We're just women of the earth, but there are women who study and perform magic more of the other realm and we think that it would be best for you to go and train with them."

"You're sending me away?!" I yell wounded.

"We are trying to help you. We want you to be able to better understand and control your powers, and there is only so much your aunt and I are capable of. This way, you will be around witches who can support you and give you the advice you need when you get these… power surges."

"And you agree with this?" I question my Aunt Gerta.

"I do," She whispers, not taking her eyes up from the ground.

I was quiet for a moment, swallowing tears. I did not want them to see how much they have hurt me with this information. When I finally felt in controlled, I glared back at my aunts, "So where are you sending me? If you reveal to me that Hogwarts has actually been real all of this time, I'm going to kill you."

"It's not Hogwarts," Lila responded with an eye roll. I heard my Aunt Gerta let a small chuckle slip out, "It's a coven. There is a group of powerful witches that has been training young witches like yourself in the woods of Massachusetts for years."

"Why Massachusetts of all places?" I snark.

"Isn't obvious," Aunt Lila adds, no longer staring at the floor. "Salem."

Of course. Salem was the witch capital of the United States. It only made sense that some secret batch of sorceresses would spring up there.

"How on earth does no one in Massachusetts no about a crazy witch coven? That seems like it would make the local news at least," I question.

"After the witch trials, a coven of witches decided that women needed a place to go where they could practice their magic in safety. They needed a haven. So, a handful of the strongest witches banded together and used their strongest magic to protect the coven from unwanted eyes. Almost all of the witches who created it died, except for one. She became the first Head of the Coven. The Head of the coven ensures that the witches in attendance are safe and that the magic that protects them never falters. Those witches made a safe place to study true magic. It really is miraculous."

Do I have to go?" I whisper, "What about school?"

"The coven will take of your schooling," Lila responds. I blink at them confused. Lila sighs, "You'll take your classes online along with your training."

I've never had a lot of friends. Most of my peers thought I was an oddball, and I've always preferred to work alone, but this was my home. I was comfortable here, and the idea of being sent away made me tingle with nervous energy.

"When do I leave?" I ask. I hoped that I would at least have a little time to process this information, maybe try and do some research about the coven on my own.

My aunts looked at one another solemnly and then turned back to me.

"Tomorrow."

CHAPTER FOUR:

DARIEN

I can't breathe. I can't see. My hands claw around the smooth surface of what I assumed to be tile below me as I try to find some answer as to where I am.

Slowly, I begin to catch my breath as specks of light started to dance around the edges of my vision.

I closed my eyes tightly and laid in a fetal position on the floor in an attempt to recollect myself. The chill of the tile was soothing and started to cool my burning flesh. Once my breathing had started to even out, I opened my eyes carefully. After taking a second to look around, I let out a sigh of relief that my vision had returned.

Now that I knew that I wasn't blind, I achingly pulled myself up to a cross-legged position and tried to identify my surroundings.

It was all vaguely familiar, like the wisps of a dream that you had just woken up from. The walls were red and black. Posters of playing cards and velvet top hats lined the walls.

Along the wall across from me, was a murky display case presenting strange artifacts such as stuffed rabbits, and masks. To me left was a pair of velvet ropes that must be used to form a line leading to a pair of bright red double doors.

A magician's theater. Delightful. If the Dark Lord wanted to see some card tricks, I could have whipped out a couple of moves and got to the point.

I chuckle to myself and my laughter turns to agony as a sharp pain rips through my chest like a hot knife. It's burning and hot and makes me double over and wheeze. With each rasp, memories start to flood my mind. The Book of Souls is inside of me. Waiting. I remember that I have a job to do, but why on Earth was I brought back to life here of all places.

The pain begins to subside and I crawl my way to the nearest wall, which I use for balance as I stand up. Every muscle in my body aches and my head is swimming, but I guide myself along the wall around the room. The more I walk, the more my shaky legs start to steady with each step, I become more familiar with my surroundings and old memories begin to resurface.

Step. I'm in a magician's theater.

Step. I was a magician. Ok magician is being generous. I was more of a scam artist with a good sleight of hand, but I worked in this theater.

Step. My real magic was with gambling and stealing.

Step. I stole from someone I was not supposed to. I can't remember who, but that is why I died.

Step. My name is Darien Burron and I have just returned from the dead.

Step. I need to find myself a witch.

I had made my way entirely around the room and was now no longer leaning against the wall, my legs had begun to find their strength again. Now that I knew that I could move, it was time to see if I was truly alone.

I made my way to the double doors and pushed. They swung open easily, revealing a dark theater. I pawed blindly in the dark for a moment until I found a light switch and flicked the lights on. The lights were not very useful, however, as they illuminated the room in feeble flickers. It was obvious that the theater had not been cleaned in months as there was a faint layer of dust along the floors and chairs. Cobwebs lined the tops of small chandeliers and as I walked towards the stage, I noticed that many of the seats were worn and tattered from lack of care.

When I arrived to the foot of the stage, I ran my hand along the edge. In a past life I had stood at the edge of this stage more times than I could count. I was not the main magician. I was one of a couple of pre-show trick artists whose jobs were to warm up the audience before the show. Gerald Gain was the main magician. He used cheap tricks, but he had a smile that lit up an entire room and a rich, deep voice like dark silk. He could charm a room to believe whatever he said. He also managed to woo many a lady back to his dressing room with that smile and voice.

Behind the scenes, Gerald had a much more lucrative business brewing. He had gathered a small group of boys, myself included. We were all the same. No parents, poor, and quick handed. He let us live at the back of the theater and provided us with food and resources. In exchange, we were his thieves.

I was just nine years old when Gerald took me in. We were just petty pick pockets when we were young. It was all very Oliver Twist. But as we got older, the wallets of the elderly were not enough. So Gerald began an elaborate gambling ring right on this very stage. Late at night, when the rest of the world slept, Gerald would invite the nastiest sort of people to the theater to gamble their fortunes and lives away. It was out job to make sure that Gerald always won.

He would integrate us into the game and with our slights of hand, we would always ensure that we won the hand. If we didn't win, would make sure to snatch the winnings away before they even left the building. Needless to say, Gerald made a lot of enemies.

But now, as I ran my finger along the edge of the stage, the layer of dust showed me that no one had been on this stage in quite a while. I was alone. I sighed deeply and flung myself up onto the stage, my footsteps booming across the room with every step I took. I strode across the creaky, wooden planks and turned stage right to make my way backstage.

I swept back the black curtain and crept past the array of props thrown haphazardly in the dark. Past a pair of dented bird cages and torn, red fabrics was a dingy, metallic door. I opened the door and gasped.

These halls that had once been filled with bustling life and laughter was empty. Along the white was were dark reddish-brown stains with a peppering of bullet holes. Furniture was knocked over, scratch marks lines the walls and floor, a lone shoe laid abandoned on the desolate floor.

I clutched my chest and gaped around the room. I could hear the firing of gunshots, the screams of my friends, the smell of blood and sweat. Panic. Frenzy. I picked up the shoe, feeling the familiar weight. When I looked down, I drops of the same reddish-brown stain ran along the floor. The memories poured over me. Blood. My blood. I followed the trail of drops back to the stage.

Without thinking, I flicked the lights to the stage and limelight. I could now see the stains growing larger as they approached the center of the stage. I followed each drop until I was fully in the center of the stage. When I had reached the end of the trail. I looked up, and was blinded by the bright limelight shining down onto my upturned face. I must have turned it on when I entered the theater.

The lights, the screams. It was all coming back to me. The memories whirled through my mind like a movie on fast forward. When it was done, I realized I had been holding my breath. I unleashed a great exhale as a tear slipped down my cheek. Gerald had died. My friends had died. This is where I died.

I gulped and roughly brushed the tear from my cheek. My old world was gone, but I had to move on. There was no way I was going to die again any time soon

CHAPTER FIVE: MIRAH

I really hope I packed enough socks. I stood in the middle of a great forest, a suitcase in each hand. The past twenty-four hours had been an absolute whirlwind. I didn't even have time to protest to my aunts for more time before I was sent into a tornado of packing, my whole life being tossed into two bags in a matter of hours.

I refused to cry in front of my aunts, though they certainly wept and apologized more than enough for me. In private though, as I kissed my sweet cat's goodbye, I couldn't help but choke out a few sobs. I was being thrown to a world I knew nothing, because of powers that I knew nothing about. I no longer had any control of my life and I was terrified.

When my aunts and I arrived at our destination the next day, instead of houses, shops, and restaurants, I was greeted to the edge of a dark, twisting wood. Both of my aunts offered to show me the way to the coven, but I begged them not to. I didn't not want people's first impression of me to be me being led in by my aunts like it was my first day of kindergarten.

Also, I knew that I was holding it together by a string and I didn't know how much longer I could make before I broke down. If I was going to do this. I needed my aunts to leave as soon as possible.

With a few final hugs and kisses, along with many promises to write, I marched my way into the cold dark wood, feeling very much like Little Red Riding Hood on her way to her grandmother's. I hope a wolf doesn't eat me along the way.

The path through the woods was very twisted. Long branches covered in ivy dangled low forcing me to keep alert so that I would not run straight into one and knock myself out. Along the ground, roots raised up scarring the ground and making me trip more times than I could count.

After about an hour, I realized that I was hungry, tired, and terribly lost. Defeated, I turned to my phone so that I could call my aunts for directions, but there was no signal to be had. Lovely.

I slumped down on a nearby rock and put my head in my hands. Then after a small squeal of frustration and a few kicks of a temper tantrum, I had just about decided to give up and to try and turn around and find my way out of these woods before I became dinner for some lurking carnivore, when I heard laughter coming from my right. I followed the sound of giggles further into woods until I started to notice small lights flickering among the trees.

At first glance, they looked like fireflies, but upon further inspection, they were actually just small orbs of light. They floated on their own among the foliage, giving a soft glow to a faded path. The more I followed the lights, the more the voices grew louder. I quickened my pace in excitement, but ended up stumbling over a gnarled root and ended up sprawling onto the ground.

The chatter had stopped and silence filled the air. When I looked up, I found that I was in the middle of a clearing. An older woman with spiraling red hair in a long black dress stood surrounded by a group of girls of various ages. All of them were dressed in black. Around the clearing the orbs of light shone brightly near the tops of the trees.

In the center of the circle there was a silver altar lined with candles that flickered in the breeze. Incense smoked into the air and I could the see the glimmer from the shine of a ceremonial knife. Two chalices stood on either side of the altar, both were made of silver with the symbol of three moons: a waxing, a waning, and a full moon. This was the symbol of the goddess of the female force in magic.

There was an awkward moment of silence and then the red-headed woman sprung towards me and helped raise me to my feet.

"Welcome sister! My name is Martha Goode. I am the Head or leader of this coven. We've been expecting your arrival and we're so happy to see you!" The red headed woman gestured to the group of girls behind her and took my arm, leading me towards the altar.

So much for my great first impression, I thought to myself. Also, it would have been nice if my aunts had told me about the all black clothing rule. I had worn my favorite blouse and leggings, but the bright yellow of my shirt made me stand out like a sore thumb.

When we got to the altar, Martha gave my arm a reassuring squeeze and handed me one of the chalices from the table.

"We're sure your very tired and you need some time to rest. But before we show you your room, we would just like to greet you to a cleansing spell. We want to help clear away any negativity you may be feeling and purge you of some stress."

She picked up the other chalice and motioned for me to follow her lead. She sipped from the cup and I did the same. The warm liquid inside tasted sweet and reminded me off eggnog with its notes of cinnamon. The more I drank, the warmer I felt. It was like submerging myself in a nice hot bath.

After I had finished the drink, I couldn't help but smile and I heard the girls around me break into a polite round of applause

Martha finished her drink and silenced the rest of the girls with a wave of her hand.

"Marvelous! She boomed, "Now that you're ready we will show you to room. Tonight, we will have a delicious dinner and then," her smile faltered a bit, "it will be time for the binding spell."

I opened my mouth to ask what a "binding spell" entailed, but most of the crowd had begun to walk away and Martha glided away swiftly before I could stop her.

"I'll show you to your room," a soft voice murmured in my ear, making me jump.

I turned to see a dark-skinned girl with large doe eyes standing beside me.

"Great," I stammer and I follow her gently swinging braid as she leads me past the clearing.

I tried introducing myself to the girl, hoping that maybe this could be the start of a new friendship, but other than the curt stating of her name, "Ariea," There was no other conversation to be had.

Past the opening, was a more clearly marked trail. After a short walk, I was met with a sight that took my breath away.

To call it a treehouse would be a grievous understatement. At the end of the path there was a cluster of trees with a staircase the wrapped around the trunk. Entangled amongst the branches were ornate silver houses that sparkled like starlight. The houses were all connected to one another by curved bridges with bright gems gleaming from the sides. It was breathtaking and it must have taken some serious magic to keep these houses secure within the forest.

Ariea poked me in the shoulder and pointed to one of the houses near the back of the collection of homes. I followed her as we walked around and around the tree up to our landing.

When we finally reached the top, I was gasping for breath, Ariea seemed unfazed by our long trek up the stairs.

Inside the house there was a sitting room with a roaring fireplace. Gorgeous velvet chairs and couches filled the room and tables were scattered around the room with books, games, magazines, star charts, makeup, potion bottles, herbs, gems, athletic equipment, papers, and pens.

Ariea brought me to a large oak door. On either side of the door two beautiful glass spheres with swirls of reds and oranges and greens and blues within. Witch Balls. We didn't sell them at the shop, but I knew of them and how they were used to protect against evil.

"That's a really nice set of balls," I commented to Ariea.

As soon as it was out of my mouth, I realized how that remark sounded. But, before I could explain myself, Ariea rolled her eyes at me and swung open the door and strutted in.

Inside was a moss colored, spacious room filled with six canopied beds. Along one wall was a row of chestnut brown dressers and a long mirror. On another wall were a few windows closed for now by think green curtains and a small white door.

"*Tneu*" Ariea stated. The soft glowing orbs from the forest floated softly upward and gently lit up the room.

"Your bed's over there," Ariea said point towards the bed farthest from the door. "Your dresser is all the way to the right and the bathroom is through that white door. Dinner is at 5:30, lunch is at noon, and breakfast is at 8:00am. It's first come first serve. If your late and there's no good food left that's on you. We take our normal school classes in the morning and then after lunch we focus on our training. After dinner we have time to do our homework, activities, or whatever we want honestly. It's up to you to get your work done."

I nod as I sit down on my new bed. It's a bit soft for my taste, but I suppose I'll have to get used to it.

"When we're not in training you can wear whatever you want, even pajamas if you really feel like it. But during training, you need to wear black. If you don't this will dismiss you for the day and you will fall behind in your training quickly," Ariea droned on.

"Where do they serve dinner," I asked curiously.

"The main cottage. It's in the center of the Hideaway. It's the biggest cottage, you won't be able to miss it. This is also where we take our online classes as it's the only place with any sort of technology."

"We're not allowed to have phones or computers in our own cottage?" I questioned.

"I mean technically, we can, but there is no internet or service in any of the other cottages, so there's really no point."

Boo. Why do witches have to be so old-fashioned. Ariea turned to leave and called to me over her shoulder, "I'll let you get unpacked. You have time to change too, if you want." She added eyeing my outfit up and down.

"Thanks…" I mutter, "Before you go, what did Martha mean by a binding spell?"

Aria spins around and looks at me bewildered, "A binding spell? It connects you to coven."

"Connects me to the coven?" I stutter.

"Well yeah." Aria's dark eyes meet mine, "It means if you need help, we'll protect you. If you betray us, we'll kill you." With that final bode of confidence Ariea turned and started making her way towards the door leaving my mouth agape.

CHAPTER SIX: DARIEN

I was so lost in my thoughts; I didn't hear the clamor of men until they were right outside the theater. The doors burst open and by instinct, I kicked up the trap door that laid in the middle of the stage and dropped to the floor of the room.

I forced myself to take deep steady breaths. I needed to control my heartbeat. I needed to stay sharp. So, with one ear against the wood above me, I scanned through the darkness to try and find anything that I could use as a weapon.

There were not many options for weaponry down here, it was mostly dust, cobwebs, and dead insects. But I managed to scope out the outline of an old sword used for a popular trick. One of us would sit in the audience and volunteer to be put into a box. Gerald would put swords through the box to make it appear that we were being stabbed. But after a few waves of a cloth, some spinning around, and a spell of utter gibberish, we would be revealed to the crowd as being safe and sound. The trick was that the box was already set up so that the swords would slide through a series of holes and would never actually touch you.

It was a popular trick, and this sword must have fallen down here when we were cleaning the stage on night. As quietly as I could, I scuttled over to the sword while trying to listen to the upcoming men. When I was able to clutch the handle, I found that the sword was absolutely filthy from being down here for who knows how long.

I swiped my finger along the edge of the blade and found that the sword was also completely dull. I certainly was not going to be doing much stabbing with this thing, but it was better than nothing at this point, and it may be enough to give someone a startle so that I could make a getaway.

The bellows of the men began to draw nearer, but thankfully, from what I could hear, I don't think any of them noticed my disappearing act.

"Which one of you morons left the light on when we left yesterday," a deep voice called out. There was a general grumble of men in response, but I noticed that I recognized that low voice.

I was trying to comb through the maze of my memory, when I started to hear the clamping of footsteps above me.

"We have one week to clean this dump up and open in time for our big show on Saturday!" That voice was so close now, but I still couldn't place it. It was all too many memories at once.

The mystery man continued, "People are not going to want to pay to sit in the dirt, and my actresses don't want to get ready next to the bloodstain of some urchin. Clean this place up pronto! The faster you work, the faster you can go home. If you laze around. I will keep you here all night if I have too!"

There was a sudden thunder of footsteps as a herd of people hustled around the stage. I sighed with relief and sank to the ground. I peered into the dark and found myself facing a small tunnel.

Of course, I thought, smacking myself in the forehead. There is a tunnel under the stage that leads to a back-dressing room. That's how we were able to disappear and reappear in shows. Maybe if I could make it to that dressing room, I can make a plan on how to get out of here.

I couldn't stand under the stage, so I had to crouch my way through blackness, waving my hand in front of me. Luckily, some deep part of me knew the way and in a matter of minutes, I felt my hand graze against splintered wood. I pressed my ear against the door, listening for any sounds of life on the other side. There was nothing to be heard, so I quietly crept open the door and tiptoed into the dressing room.

The dressing room was only slightly more lit then the bottom of the stage, but it was the most pristine out of any of the rooms so far. A red couch laid against the right wall and a vanity table stood across the way. I remember this used to be the room we hung out in between practices.

The lot of us would play cards, smoke, and just shoot the shit. I used to have my best times in this room.

I shook my head, trying to shake the nostalgia away. There was no time to reminisce. During my short trek in the tunnel, I recalled that down the right hall was an emergency exit that was supposed to be used in case of fires. It would set off an alarm when you opened it, but at least I would have the chance to get out of the building and make a run for it.

Again, I leaned against the door, waiting for any sign of noise. With great relief, I didn't hear anything, and I assumed that everyone was busy working on the stage. I inched open the door, just a crack and looked left to right. Nothing.

I slipped out the door and slunk silently down the hall, holding my breath the whole way down the hall. Grateful that I had always been soft-footed.

After what felt like a mile, I finally reached the end of the hall and saw the emergency exit door. I took a deep breath, readying myself to sprint as soon as the door was open. My adrenaline spiked as I flung open the door and bolted my way out. I could hear the ear-piercing wail of the fire alarm behind me as a I ran, but I knew I couldn't look back.

I savored the brisk wind against my face as I ran. I was starting to feel truly alive again. I passed the trash cans and was just about to make the corner around the building and onto the main road, when something grabbed me by the scruff of my neck, sending my flying backwards onto my rear.

Dazed with pain, my eyes struggled to focus, but I could hear the deep, rich tones of a baritone murmuring to me.

"Well who do we have here?"

It was the voice from earlier, and as I turned to look around, I felt the hand tighten around my neck.

"I wouldn't be moving around too quick if I were you boy. You and I are going to have a nice leisurely chat. All I need from you is for you to focus on the sound of my voice."

The sound of his voice. Suddenly, I was reminded of where I had heard that voice before, and a shiver ran down my spine. The memories rushed forward, the bright lights, the shouting of men, and a dark voice calling to me, telling me to look them in the eye before I died. Then there was the crack of gunshot.

I know where I died, and now I was trapped with the man who killed me.

CHAPTER SEVEN:

MIRAH

Before I had time to register if I was selling my soul to the devil. The shrieking sound of laughter bounced of the stairway and three girls jostled into the room; blocking Ariea's path. In the middle of the trio, was a stunning, statuesque, Asian girl who I immediately took to be the leader of the pack. On her right was a muscular, pixie-haired blonde and to her left was a petite brunette with large dark eyes.

"Ariea are you scaring the newbie?" The Asian girl cackled.

Ariea opened her mouth to respond, but she didn't get a chance to get a word in edgewise when the blonde interrupted her.

"Don't let her scare you. She doesn't realize how intimidating she makes everything sound." The blonde laughed and threw her arm around Ariea giving her a warm squeeze.

"She doesn't know who we are," a tiny voice chirped out and all attention was focused on the dark-eyed brunette.

"Oh my God. Duh. We're the worst," The Asian girl giggled. She then straightened her face and adjusted her posture to give herself the facade of false propriety.

"My name is Mai," She began putting her palm to her chest and flashing me the whitest smile I have ever seen.

"This is Tamara," Mai gestured to the blonde. At this introduction Tamara gave an enthusiastic wave, "And the tiny one over here is Elaina." Mai continued. Elaina gave a small, polite nod.

"Of course, you have already been introduced to Aria and her sparkling personality," Mai gestured to Aria and Tamara gave her another squeeze as Aria stood there and scowled.

"We welcome you to our coven!" Mai shouted and Tamara and Elaina broke out in a courteous round of applause.

"Uh. Thanks," I grunted, very much overwhelmed by the rapid events that was occurring.

"I know you're overwhelmed by the rapid events that have been occurring, but I promise you, you'll get used to it soon," Elaina murmured.

I stared at her bewildered, and Mai elbowed her in the side, "Now you're freaking her out. Mai chuckled and turned to me, "Elaina our resident clairvoyant."

"So, she can read my mind," I asked nervously.

"She's gotten really good at managing it," Tamara explained, "I think she's just excited to meet you and she's just trying to feel you out."

"I've gotten to the point where I can tune the noises out. It's usually just a unreadable hum in the background, but when I meet new people, their internal voice is much sharper and I need to get to know them a bit better, before they become my brain's background noise. Sorry if I creeped you out."

I blink stunned at the girls. My aunts knew some small tricks. Minor spells for healing or for cleansing a room, and they would turn to Tarot cards from time to time, but this was my first-time meeting someone with actual powers.

"So, everyone here can do actual magic?" I asked.

"Yuppers!" Mai yelled, "Usually we're not quite as focused as Elaina is, but we can throw around some hocus pocus."

I look down nervously. I've never purposely shown any real impressive magic. I was good with palm reading and I could mix up some mean herbs, but the kind of magic these girls were talking about sounded a lot more impressive than poking at hands and lighting up some lavender.

On top of that, the only instances when I displayed any real power, I had no control over it. I look down at my hands and slump on the bed. The lump in my throat making it impossible to swallow. I didn't belong here. At best they were going to realize quickly that I was a hack, or at worst, I was really going to hurt someone.

I feel the bed sag as Tamara sits next to me, "Hey are you Okay?"

I nod, but I can feel the tears rushing to my eyes.

"Listen," Mai adds sitting on the other side of me, "Everyone feels homesick at first. It's totally normal, but after a while everything's going to be just fine. Right ladies."

Tamara and Elaina echo their agreements. Aria nods but I can see her looking out the doorway, tapping her foot impatiently.

"Why don't we give her some space, Elaina whispers, "She's going through a lot right now."

I open my mouth to argue, but Mai and Tamara were already on their way out, calling out reassurances every step of the way. Aria left so quickly I didn't see her disappear.

In a second, they were gone just as quick as they appeared and I was left alone with my thoughts. I breathed deeply, feeling the tears coming unbidden again to my eyes. Other than for a few sleepovers, I had never been away from home before. I missed my cats, I missed my leather chair, I missed my aunts. I thought about putting my things away in my closet, but my too soft bedding was much more tempting. In moments I had fallen asleep with only a couple of tear stains on my pillow.

***

I was woken up later by a small shake in my shoulder. I rolled over sleepily to see Elaina's wide dark eyes staring back at me.

"Dinner's in a half an hour if you want to get ready," She murmured.

I nodded my thanks and Elaina moved over to her bed and began to braid her long hair while humming softly to herself.

After a few seconds of procrastination, I dragged myself out of bed. I must have slept for a couple of hours as it was now quiet dark except for the glow of soft orbs dancing around the room.

After a short shower, I stood shivering in front of my luggage trying to pick out an outfit for the night. I wanted something that said, cool but not trying to hard, and totally not freaked out at the idea of selling her soul to some mysterious witch coven.

I grabbed a black wrap dress and clomped my way down the stairs and out the the door. I looked around the outside and I took in the beauty of my surroundings. In the twilight, the houses in the trees illuminated a peaceful white light and fireflies danced around the grass and wildflowers. All I wanted to do was grab a book and hide away in this serene picture, but my stomach grumbled and I was reminded that I needed to grab dinner.

I started walking more towards the middle of the space and found that Ariea was not kidding when she said that the main house would be easy to find.

Perched on a gigantic oak tree was an enormous structure entangled in the branches and leaves. Unlike the soft glow that the silver houses displayed, this building was made of glittering gold that sparkled and danced in the starlight.

I was gaping open mouthed at the wondrous sight when I felt two arms wrap around my shoulders forcing me forward.

"Hurry up or all the good stuff will be gone!" Tamara shrieked.

"We'll show you more around tomorrow after class!" Mai chirped. I heard a small chuckle and turned around to find Elaina trotting along behind us.

With Tamara and Mai on either side of me, I was marched towards the entrance of the Main Hall. The main doors were massive with intricate images of the stages of the Goddess. A chubby cheeked young woman to represent the maid. An ethereal woman with flowing hair, belly curved with child, to represent the mother. To the right was a crooked elderly woman clutching a crutch that must have been the crone hand carved into its wood.

Tamara swung open the door and dragged me into a marvelous marble foyer. The images of the goddess still stood before me, but now as three golden statues next to three hallways.

Tamara took and abrupt right and I was led down a spacious hallway filled with art that ranged from old to modern and from cheerful to macabre. At the end of the hallway was the dining room with walls of dark wood and golden candlelight flickering from the three long tables that filled the room.

In the center of the room was a dark, deep pit that seemed to go on forever surrounded by ancient stone. Tamara told me this was simply called the portal and it was only used for some of the most difficult ceremonies.

"Just keep an eye for it," Mai remarked, "You don't want to not be paying attention and then take a tumble down that thing. There's no telling how far that thing goes."

I was plunked down at a seat between Tamara and Mai and gaped around the table. Rich plates of food lined one end of the table to another. I was lost to the chorus of girls laughing and the tinkling of silverware, when a piece of meat was flashed before my face.

"You have got to try the chicken. It's delicious tonight," Mai insisted.

"If you don't eat meat there are other options too." Elaina added, twirling up some form of pasta.

"I'll eat anything," I managed to sputter. The girls grinned and I found myself grinning back at them. It was the first time I had smiled all day, and I felt my muscles start to loosen and the knot in my stomach start to lesson. Maybe I would be able to make some friends here.

Not wanting to miss a thing, I stacked up an impressive pile of food onto my plate and was munching along and enjoying listening to the sporadic conversation of new spells and failed potions. I was laughing at Mai's story about a tree frog and a Ouija board when I suddenly locked eyes with Martha from earlier.

She beamed at me. I smiled back, but as Martha's hazel eyes lingered on my pale eyes, I saw her smile falter for just a second before I looked away.

It was only a moment, but it was enough to remind me that I didn't belong here. I wasn't special. I was becoming frightening and maybe she was figuring that out. Maybe at this ceremony, they'll learn about the darkness inside me and throw me out. More importantly, what was I getting myself into?

Did I really want to bind myself to this coven? I barely knew anything about this organization. I was just sent here by the whims of my aunts. What if this turns out to be something I regret. What if I mess up without even knowing it and then I have a crazed band of witches trying to take me out. What if…

I was so lost in the spiral of my thoughts, that I didn't even hear the conversation that was going on around me.

"Mirah?" a voice called out.

I shook my head and looked around to try and find who had called my name.

"Mirah, did you hear me?" Mai asked her head on her hand, eyeing me curiously.

"Sorry, what did you say?" I questioned.

"I was just saying that we've been rude all dinner and we've been talking, but we haven't even asked you about yourself. So, I'm trying to remedy that. So… Tell us about yourself."

Suddenly all eyes were on me and I didn't even know where to begin. In my old school I had a small collection of people I talked to and ate lunch with, but I never considered them friends. We never slept over at each other's houses or called each other after school.

Growing up with two lesbian aunts who ran a Witch store in the heart of Pennsatucky, PA didn't exactly make me popular. I learned to hide in the background and I always tried to appear as non-descriptive as a possible.

Now my commonness was a hindrance as I found that I had nothing interesting to say about myself, especially in front of these dazzling girls.

I was desperately trying to think of something interesting to say, when I was saved by the clinking of metal against glass.

"Ladies," Martha boomed out, sweeping the long sleeve of her robe around the room, "I hope you have enjoyed your supper."

There were the general noises of consensus, which were soon silenced by an upturned hand.

"Wonderful. Take this time to savor your meals and relax. After dinner we will be welcoming a new member to our sisterhood." Martha gestured towards me and there was a polite round of applause, and I noticed Martha's smile did not meet her eyes.

With another wave of her hand, Martha silenced the girls, "Mirah will be joined to us through our coven's binding spell. It is what connects all of us as sisters. It it an eternal bond," She added with grave seriousness, "But for now, eat, drink, and help Mirah feel at home!"

There was a moment of silence, followed by some scattered applause, but most of the girls had quickly returned to their conversations.

"No one has told me what this binding spell entails," I asked searching to the girls around me.

"It's really not that big of a deal," Tamara reassured me.

"Tamara's right," Mai interjected, "Martha just likes for everything, and I do mean everything, to be as dramatic as possible."

"What will I have to do?" I wondered.

"You really don't have to do much," Mai remarked, "The coven ends up doing most of the work for you."

"We'll go to the field where we meet you earlier," Tamara explained, "We will then form a circle around you while you stand in the middle. There some stuff you have to say, but you just have to repeat after Martha, so it's not like you have to have anything memorized."

"What will I have to say," I interjected.

"Oh, some babble about being faithful to the coven," Tamara answered waving my question away.

"Do I have to do this?" I asked. It's not that I was against joining this coven. It just would have been nice to have some time to think about it.

"Well, no," Tamara said with confusion.

"But if you don't perform the spell, you can't stay here." Mai sniped, suddenly serious.

Did I even want to stay? A large part of me wanted to go home to my comfortable life. But, I couldn't deny that there was something about this place that excited me. I made me feel like I was becoming part of something bigger than myself, something important.

My thoughts were broken by the clinking of glass once again. This time the girls were much quicker in getting silent.

Martha stood at the front of the dining hall and motioned for the girls to start to rise.

"Ladies, I hope you have enjoyed your meal. You should start to make your way to the Sanctuary. It is time."

Quietly, the girls started to make their way out of the dining hall in a single file. Tamara nudged me in the rib and I started to follow the girls outside. It looks like I had to make a decision and I had to make it now.

CHAPTER EIGHT:

DARIEN

Thomas McLindon was the name of the man who killed me, and based on current events, it looked like he was going to get to kill me again.

I was dragged back into the theater by the scruff of my neck and thrown into a nearby chair. McLindon motioned to some of his crew that they should tie me up. In a matter of seconds I was tied up in series of poorly knotted ropes.

McLindon was a gang member with a very serious gambling problem. He had come to Gerald's poker nights many times and had lost himself countless amounts of cash. One night though, he actually won, but Gerald refused to pay up. They got into a knockdown, drag out fight about it and he was eventually banned from the gambling ring. Apparently, he did not take to kindly to this. As he ordered a hit on all of us.

"Get out!" McLindon barked, "I want to talk to this piece of scum alone."

The men hurried out until it was just McLindon and I facing one another. I tugged on the ropes. As a magician's assistant, I was not unfamiliar with the art of knots. McLindon's men needed more practice.

I began working on my bonds as McLindon paced back and forth across the room until he settled himself on the edge of the seat across from me.

"I know you boy. You were one of Gerald's lackeys" McLindon began.

"I prefer the term employee, but otherwise you are correct," I snarked. What was the worse this guy could do to me? Kill me? Please, been there done that. If I was going to get murdered again, at least I was going to go out with a little bit of fun.

"Don't sass me boy," McLindon snarled. His face suddenly darkened and he inched closer to me.

"I also know that you were dead," He whispered, "I was there. I killed you myself. I saw you bleed on that stage."

"Also correct," I retorted. Secretly sliding my hands out of the ropes. Working for a magician did have some perks, the rest of the ties would be easy to unravel now.

"How the hell are you here then," McLindon growled, but I could see traces of real fear in his eye.

"Magic," I hissed. As the last strands of the rope fell away. I lunged at McLindon, knocking him backwards off the chair to the floor.

I had originally just planned to surprise him and knock him around so that I could escape, but as we wrestled on the ground, I felt a rage grow unbidden inside of me. I wrapped my hands around his throat and felt start to grow warm.

I pressed tighter, my vision growing white and my fingertips started to burn. I could hear McLindon's screams but something inside of me wouldn't let go. I pressed tighter and tighter. The hands pouring out of my hands.

Finally, the screams stopped and I felt the body slump in my hands. I stood up and stepped back out of breath, tripping into the chair that I was once tied in.

As my vision started to return, I saw what was left of McLindon. He was very tall, but thin, so as he laid on the ground, he looked like a marionette doll that had been thrown aside. His neck was red and dark burn marks in the shape of my fingerprints were wrapped around his neck.

I looked at my hands in horror. I had done some nasty things before, but I had never killed anyone.

I told myself not to look, but I couldn't stop myself from turning back to stare at the body. The more I looked, the more I could see small wisps of smoke floating from the burns on his neck.

I switched between glances at McLindon to my hands, unable to comprehend what had happened. My hands, though still a bit red, looked otherwise the same. What was happening? I thought, and more importantly, what am I going to do now.

The theater was still teeming with McLindon's men, who would not be pleased when they found out about what had befallen their boss. I could try and make a run for it again. This time I would probably be able to get away, but now that I had a second to think about it, a realization dawned on me.

Even if I managed to run away from the theater, where would I go? I had no place to stay, no family or friends to speak of, and no money. I was screwed.

A peal of laughter sounded from the outside and I, instinctively ducked in a corner, but no one entered the room, and I could hear the laughter and rumble of men's voices and they traveled down the hallway.

Suddenly, a voice came unbidden inside of my head and began to whisper seductively. *Kill the rest of them. It would be easy. Just sneak up on one with a gun and then finish the rest...* No. I thought, shaking my head, but the voice hissed on. *It would be justice. They killed your people, you kill theirs.* I'm not that kind of person, I mentally argued, but the voice rose causing an aching in my head. *Take their money and take the theater. It's survival.*

"No!" I yelled aloud and a searing pain spread across my forehead, making me crumble to the ground clutching my head. My eyes were closed in misery and there was a rushing in my ears. I opened my mouth to yell, but no sound came out. My fingernails dug into my scalp and I knew for sure my head would explode at any minute. But as quickly as the agony started, it ceased.

My vision returned, my voice returned, the only reminder of the torture was was a faint, but steady throbbing of my head.

I need to get out of here, I decided. Anything would be better than staying in this place. Trembling, I raised myself to my feet and made my way to the door. I swung open the door, not caring at this point anymore about discretion, ready to face whatever new challenge would be on the other side of that door.

When I stepped into the hall, I was met with silence and a strong, smoky smell. I covered my nose and coughed. As I choked, I was left wondering if the theater had caught on fire. Since I didn't hear anything, I couldn't repress my curiosity and crept my way down the hall.

As I walked, I passed small piles of ash, still wafting steam, but all of the furniture was still untouched. I grew more and more confused with each step, until I noticed a hat tossed haphazardly next to a pile of fresh ash and smoke.

Then it hit me like a ton of bricks. I knew why it was suddenly so quiet. They were burned, disintegrated. Every man that had been in here was gone.

I looked down at my palms in horror. Had I done this? How? I felt my breath start to hitch, and my throat start to tighten, when a growl of a voice echoed through the theater.

"Don't give yourself so much credit," it grumbled.

I turned around, trying to find the source of the voice.

"Who's there I cried."

From the shadows slunk an incredibly pale man. His skin was so translucent, you could see the blue of his veins on his face and neck. What little hair he had was white and faint hanging around him like a faded halo. The only color on the man's whole face was his eyes, which looked like two bulging, red-hot pieces of coal.

When I saw him, he was sitting business-like crossed legged on a chair, but as he made his way towards me. I noticed that he was small, but wiry. The gray suit that he wore hung off him like extra skin.

"Who are you?" I asked.

"My name is Jude Morow," he responded calmly, "I have been sent by my master to assist you in your task, and apparently, it was good that I got here when I did. You are in desperate need of my help."

I stared at this man. The name meant nothing to me, but there was something about this fellow that seemed familiar to me.

Suddenly it hit me, I remembered where I had seen those hideous eyes before. It was from the slug creature that had approached me in purgatory. I stepped back repulsed and surprised.

"You did this?" I questioned, motioning to the small piles simmering around me.

"Well something had to be done," he drawled." "We don't have time to worry about running away from a pack of goons. So… I took matters into my own hands."

"What are you?" I pressed disturbed at his blasé attitude towards mass murder.

"I am what my master makes me. For right now, I am your aide and your watcher."

"My watcher?!" I sputtered, "I don't need to be watched!"

"Oh, but you do. You see, as long as you carry that master's book within you," he added pointing a long, pale finger at my chest, "you will need someone to keep an eye on you."

The book. I pressed my hand against my chest and felt the heat burning inside of me. I looked back down at my hands. Realizing where the burning in my hands was coming from, and also why there was such a new rage burning inside of me.

"Yes, the book helped you kill that man. But the desire was in you first," Jude drawled.

"What are you talking about?" I pressed

"The book can bring you your most inner desires. It takes whatever deep secret wish you have within you and it brings it to the surface. So, like it or not, the book didn't make you kill that man. It just helped you bring about what you wanted."

"I'm not a murderer!" I shouted, but I felt my whole-body tremble.

"Tell that to the body back there," Jude chuckled, pointing his chin behind me.

I stared at him enraged, but Jude ignored me and grabbed a broom. He began sweeping the ash away and hummed to himself. After a few moments, he looked back at him and tossed me another broom.

"Are you going to stand there all day, or are you going to help me clean the place up," He called.

"What?" I spat.

"We need a place to stay and a fortress to plan. This will work eventually work nicely, but not with all of this filth around."

"We can't stay here," I argued, "The police will kick us out."

"If the police come, we will take care of it," Jude responded running his finger along a dusty shelf and shaking his head.

"What about money? Food?" I insisted, "I don't exactly have a secret inheritance waiting for me."

"For now, I will worry about the police and money," Jude added picking up a charred wallet from a pile of ash and dusting it off. "You need to worry about ensnaring your witch."

"That's another thing," I remarked as a dawning realization hit me, "I don't even know what this girl looks like. I don't know her name. How am I supposed to find her?"

Jude sighed deeply, annoyed at the interruptions to his sweeping, "At noon tomorrow, go to the Winegin Bridge by the edge of the Beldame forest. You will find your girl there. The rest will be on you."

"If you know so much already, why do you need me to get his girl. Why didn't your master just send you and be done with it? Why did he need to involve me?"

Jude paused, and looked up from his tidy work, "In the wheel of fate every cog plays a part. You will find your purpose at the end."

I stared at him with confusion, but Jude just gave me a knowing smile and threw a dust rag at me, "Hustle up boy. There's work to do and we have no time to lose."

CHAPTER NINE:

MIRAH

We approached the Sanctuary in silence. The field had a much different atmosphere at night. The dancing orbs were replaced by a ring of candles, which danced and flickered in the night breeze. In the dark, the trees were just outlines of twisting shadows against the firelight.

It was a New Moon and cloudy, so there was no starlight to be seen. Calmly, the girls encircled the field behind the candles. Their faces turned nightmarish by the glow of the candlelight.

There was a gentle tug on my arm. It was Martha, her red hair spiraling out of her hood was the only giveaway to her identity in the darkness. She pulled me to the center of the ring and I felt my heart start to pound.

Once Martha and I were in the middle of the circle, she raised her arms over her head.

"Sisters!" She cried, "On this glorious night, we have the joy and responsibility of bringing a new witch into our coven. New sister, speak your name.

"Uh, Mirah Bishop," I answered. The girls around me answered in a chorus of words that I did not understand, but I felt my skin begin to buzz.

"Mirah," Martha intoned, "By joining our coven, you will be entering a world of learning and wonder. Do you agree to this?"

"Sure," I blurted out. I was still unsure if I wanted to be a part of this, but wonder and learning didn't sound so bad.

"Mirah," Martha continued, "By joining our coven, you will be entering a world of kindred ship and isolation. Do you agree to this?"

"Yes," I answered even though none of what she just said made sense to me. The tingle of my skin started to become a hum.

"Mirah," Martha now shouted to the crowd, "By joining this coven, you will be entering a world of loyalty and ache. Do you agree to this?"

The ache part made me hesitant. I was always taught by my aunts to read contracts fully before I signed anything away. This felt a lot like a contract that I was skimming over.

"Mirah, do you agree," Martha pressed.

I looked around at the stony figures around me. A large part of me said I should wait. That I should get more information before I agreed to something so serious. But, a deep part of me, nestled low in my gut was pulling towards this coven. I wanted to learn more. I wanted to be a part of something special, and I had to admit to myself, I wanted the power.

With a deep breath I turned back to Martha, searching for her eyes in the dark, "I do," I answered I felt the blood rush in my veins.

Martha was silent for a moment, but then she nodded and reached towards the altar beside her. She picked up a dagger, it's blade shimmering and grabbed my hand. She turned it so that my palm was facing upwards.

Martha held the dagger aloft and began to intone a spell in a language I had never heard before. Around me, the girls followed Martha's lead chanting and hissing. My blood felt like it was starting to bubble and boil. I suddenly feared that my powers would escape me. *Keep it together,* I willed myself.

The chanting started to crescendo and I felt my breath start to shorten.

"Mirah," Martha screamed, "With this oath you become bound to this coven. You are ours and we are yours. If you need us, we will aide you. If we need you, you will aide us. You will share in happiness and despair. If a sister betrays you, they are dead to you. If you betray a sister, you are dead to us. Do you swear it?! Do you make the oath?!"

My tongue felt thick in my mouth; a white tunnel started to creep around the edges of my vision. *No. Not now. Please.* I thought.

I heard myself whisper, a single "Yes." I had no control; it was like I had become possessed.

Martha turned around the circle, the edge of the dagger facing the girls. Then she held her right pointer finger up, the witch's finger, and slide the blade down the index of her finger. Her blood trickled down her wrist making droplets on the ground.

"So, it is sworn," She cried and she pulled my hand towards me glided the blade against my own finger. I felt myself wince and try to draw away in pain, but Martha held me steady.

Once the cut was made, she pressed her finger against mine. My head started to pound, there was a roaring in my ears.

"Tonight, we are all bound!" Martha screamed, "Tonight we are a coven standing tall! We are sisters joined by one force. So, mote it be!" I heard the hateful whispers in my ears. I felt the energy rushing through me. *Please no.* I mentally begged, *I'm not going to hurt anyone.*

"So, mote it be!" called Martha to the crowd.

"So, mote it be," the girls echoed back. With that, the candles around the field extinguished. I watched the smoke drift towards the clouds until the world truly became dark for me and I fainted.

* * *

I woke up the next morning feel sore and befuddled. I was tucked neatly into my emerald green sheets. My phone and a glass of water stood beside me which I drank greedily.

Next to the water was a small note. When I read it, I saw that it from Martha. It was short, mainly suggesting that I get some rest and explore the grounds. Thankfully, I would be starting classes tomorrow.

I sighed and sunk deeper into my pillows. The events of last night spiraled through my brain. Humiliated at my behavior from the night before, I rolled over onto my stomach and clutched my pillow to my mouth, unleashing a little scream. Why couldn't I ever just be normal?

After pouting for a few minutes, I finally forced myself to get out of bed. I would eventually look around the grounds, but for right now, I needed to get away. I needed to collect myself and I wanted to see what was outside this forest hideaway.

I grabbed my wallet and hurried out of my room, relieved that no one was around. They must be at their classes, I thought. I made my way through the garden and past the Sanctuary. I looked down at my finger which had been wrapped up, but I noticed that it still throbbed from last night.

I found my way to the path and eased my way out of the forest. It was much easier getting out of the forest then it was getting to coven, even though it was the same trail, which I found odd, but I breathed a sigh of relief when I saw the parting of the trees and made my way to the outside world.

Outside the forest was a patch of some wild grass and flowers that would eventually lead to a tiny creek at the edge of a small town. I marched through the grass. I had no idea where I wanted to go, I just knew the I needed to get away for a little bit.

Once I made my way through the grass, I heard the rustling of civilization and a faint rustling of water. Separating the town from the wild was a sweet, wooden bridge.

I walked to the middle of the bridge and rested my arms along the railing. Usually, I preferred being alone, but this was the first time in my life that I felt truly lonely. I didn't belong at home with my aunts and I didn't belong with this coven. I'm dangerous and I don't know what to do.

I felt the lump in my throat start to tighten and tears threatened to spill out of my eyes. *No*, I thought. *I will not cry. I am going to pull myself together and make the best out of this. Suck it up Mirah.*

With that mental pep talk in mind, I turned to cross the bridge, accidentally knocking into a man along the way.

When I had made my way across the bridge, I heard a voice calling behind me.

"Excuse me Ma'am" is this yours?"

I turned around to see a guy around my age holding my wallet. I patted my pockets and realized that at some point my wallet must have dropped out of my pocket.

I thanked the boy profusely and as I neared him; I couldn't help noticing how handsome he was. He was tall and tan, with dark curly hair. When I got closer, I noticed he had brilliant honey-brown eyes and a strong straight nose.

I had found people attractive before, boys and girls, but I had never really given much thought to any of them. There was never anyone who interested me enough to want to further a relationship.

But as he reached out to hand me my wallet, I stared at his hands. There were strong with long graceful fingers, that made me blush.

I could feel the heat rising to my face as I pulled my hand away, but there was a deeper urge within me that I couldn't ignore. This guy was going to be mine.

"Thank you so much," I grinned up at him.

"No problem," He smiled back at me. His teeth white and straight against tan skin, "It was on the bridge, it must have fallen as you were crossing over."

"I can't thank you enough," I tried to giggle like I had seen the girls in movies do, but I accidentally choked a bit on my own spit and began a small coughing fit.

"I'm happy to help," he answered, but looked at me with concern as I tried to stifle my hacks, "Are you okay?"

"Fine, yeah, sorry," I wheezed out feeling my face growing even redder. I took a couple deep breaths to try and compose myself and straightened, hoping that I hadn't ruined my chances.

"I just need something to drink," I laughed, "How about I buy you a coffee to thank you for saving my wallet." I went to affectionately grab him by the arm, but ended up just kind of, awkwardly slugging him in the arm like I was one of his bros. It was all very smooth.

He grinned wider and his eyes began to sparkle, "That sounds perfect," he smirked, "Where would you like to go."

"That's an issue," I responded, feeling more idiotic by the second, "I'm new around here, so I don't really know where anything is."

"Well, in that case," he answered looking mischievous, "let me show you around a bit, and then you can get me a nice expensive, cup of coffee."

He gave me a playful slug on the shoulder and motioned for me to follow him. My heart sped up as I hurried to follow him, having to take two steps for every one of his long strides.

"So, Sir," I chirped, "since you are to be my tour guide for now, I should probably tell you my name. I'm Mirah Bishop." I held out my hand for him to shake.

He stopped and turned grabbing my hand. He hand was warm and something start to ignite in me, the sparks of a flame. He gave my hand one good solid shake and answered,

"Darien Burron"

CHAPTER TEN: DARIEN

Jude was right. It was not hard to find the witch. After spending hours yesterday cleaning the theater and being bossed around by Jude, I was relieved this morning to get away. For a demon, Jude had some very strong feelings about curtains.

I had followed Jude's orders and made my way to the Ginwhiskey Bridge, which I had not been to since I was a child.

She was already there when I arrived, leaning against the bridge, her long wavy hair dangling over the edge. I didn't know her name, or even what she looked like when I set out for my morning adventure, but as soon as I saw her, I knew immediately that she would be my witch.

She was small, but the energy around her was electric. The closer I got to her, the more I felt a pull in my chest leading me towards her.

It was painfully easy to get her attention. As she passed me on the bridge, I swiped her wallet quick as can be. Now we were heading for coffee and I was a white knight in her mind, or at least hoped to be by the end of the day.

With each hour I remembered more and more about the past. I led her through the town to a cozy little cafe at the corner of town that I recalled that I used to enjoy.

As we walked, I pointed out the different stores and landmarks, making sure to casually brush up against her as much as I could. It was usually easy to tell when a girl was having a good time and was smitten, but Mirah was difficult to read. Other than some slight blushing, her face remained calm and neutral and I wondered what I would have to do to get any real emotion out of this girl.

When we had reached the entrance to the cafe, I swung open the door and motioned her inside. Girls always loved this cafe. It was small and modern with herbs as centerpieces on the tables and different art mosaics throughout the building.

Along with coffee, this place also had a wide arrange of sweets from cupcakes to brownies that were homemade on the premises. As she read the menu, I peeked out of the corner of my eye to observe this mysterious witch.

She was cute, with a perky little nose speckled with freckles, and cool, blue eyes. However, other than her strong aura, there was nothing particularly unusual about this girl, which I thought was odd. I mean, if the devil is going through all of this trouble to try and ensnare this girl, you would think that maybe she would have a little more zing to her.

We placed our orders and, even though I offered to pay, she insisted on buying. So, with our steaming drinks in hand, we made our way to a private table next to a stunning mosaic of blacks, silvers, and grays.

I looked at those cool blue-green eyes and wondered what exactly I was supposed to do. I mean, I know that I have to get this girl to sign the devil's book, but it's not like the King of Darkness handed me an instructional manual, and all Jude told me was to meet this girl at the bridge. Why did the King of Darkness want this girl so bad? How was I supposed to get this girl to sign his book? How was I going to even get this thing out of me?

"Are you okay?"

I started and looked back at Mirah who was staring at me with confusion.

"Oh, yeah. Sorry. I haven't been getting much sleep lately, so I've been zoning out a bit." It wasn't a total lie. I hadn't really gotten a good night's rest since before I died, so that can do a lot to a person.

"Insomnia? I used to have that really bad a few years ago," She replied.

"No…" I hesitated trying to think of what to say, "I used to work at a theater. The old manager… passed away and bequeathed it to me. So now I'm trying to prepare it for its reopening."

"Wow! That's amazing!" Mirah exclaimed, "So are you some kind of actor?"

"Magician," I grinned slyly. Girls love magic. I could convince her to come see a show, and then at least I could make sure that I see her again. This time it would be on my own turf to.

"Magician?" She chuckled to herself and looked at me mischievously, "Can you show me any tricks?"

"Sure," I grinned, "Do you have a coin?"

She slid\a quarter towards me. I picked it up and twirled it between my fingers, "Watch closely, my dear, for before your very eyes, I am going to make this coin disappear."

It was a terribly easy trick and was actually one of the first tricks I ever learned. The key was to put the coin on your middle and ring finger and you pretend to put the coin in your other hand. However, you curve your fingers so that the coin never moves. To the observer, it looks like you passed the coin to your other hand, so when you open your palm it looks like the coin had disappeared.

As I wiggled my fingers before her to show her the "missing" coin, she laughed. Her laugh was soft and musical and I found myself wanting to impress her more so that I could hear that laugh again.

I made the coin "reappear" and handed it back to her. She gave me a polite golf clap, but saw a twinkle in her eye has if she were keeping a secret.

"You know," Mirah whispered as she leaned across the table, "I know a little magic too."

"Oh, do you," I chuckled, but I felt my chest tighten. I must admit, I had never believed in real magic before. When Jude told me that I needed to hunt down a witch, I didn't think too much about it, but now that I was across from her, I realized that if the darkness itself was willing to hunt this girl down. She must have some actual powers.

"I showed you a trick. Now it's your turn," I teased. I wanted to see a taste of what actual magic looked like, not just my sleight of hand. I wanted to see real power. Could she turn people into toads? Fly on a broom? I was desperate to know.

She giggled and twirled the wrapper for her straw around in her hands. It's not the kind of magic that you can see right away. At least, I can't do that kind of magic yet," She murmured.

"What kind of magic can you do," I pressed, somewhat disappointed.

"It's a bit more subtle," A tiny smile curled around the edges of her lips, but I could tell that she was not going to give me any more information for now.

"So, when you're not practicing your special magic, what do you like to do? Do you live around here?"

"My… school is around here," She replied, "It's a… girls boarding school in a way."

"How Victorian," I smirked, "Do they teach you how to curtsy?"

"Of course," she responded with false primness, "I still have a lot of work to do in the curtsy department, but boy do I know how to work a fan."

"Impressive." I snicker, "When you're not learning the fine arts of being a lady, what do you like to do?"

"Oh, read, write, yoga. Quiet activities mainly," Mirah sighed.

"Yoga," I pressed.

"Oh yes," She smirked, "I'm not that graceful, but I am rather limber," she added with a waggle of her eyebrows.

Before I could respond, she looked at the large clock hanging next to the menu and sighed, "Speaking of school, I should start to head back. People may be starting to look for me."

"Do you have a curfew?" I wondered.

"Yes and no," She answered and started to clean up her drink.

"One more trick before you go," I asked.

I grabbed her straw wrapper that she had torn into shreds as we were talking. I held the shreds in the palm of my hand and motioned for her to watch. Slowly, I closed my fist and whispered a little gibberish as I wrapped my other fist around my hand. As I whispered, I traded the shredded pieces of paper for my own wrapper.

It appeared, when I opened my palm, that I put her wrapper back together through magic. She laughed and clapped again, more enthusiastically this time. I laughed back, but I felt my throat drop to the pit of my stomach.

I knew who she was now, and I had to make sure that she didn't get away.

"So when can I see you again," I pressed, "I can show you some actually impressive magic next time."

She looked up at me and tilted her head taking me in and making me. As her eyes scanned me over, I felt sweat start to bead on my chest and I couldn't even guess what she was thinking.

Finally, she nodded and slide the receipt for the drinks towards me and grabbed a pen from the counter.

"Give me your number and I'll call you," She said calmly.

"You know it's usually the guy who takes the girl's number," I joked.

"True. But, first of all, the phone situation at my school is complicated, so it's easier if I call you. Second, you'll come to find that I'm not one for traditions. I prefer to make things work my own way."

I gave her the number for the theater, as I did not have a personal phone on me for the moment. As I handed, her the receipt, I felt the energy between us ignite again. Static filled the air and I could feel the hair on my arms stand upright as goosebumps rippled through my body. I looked down at the receipt and noticed that the corners were starting to singe and curl.

"Thanks," she squeaked, and before I could say anything else, I watched open-mouthed as she hurried out of the cafe with the faint smell of smoke trailing behind her.

CHAPTER ELEVEN:

MIRAH

Once I knew that I was out of Darien's sight, I squealed and jogged towards the forest clearing. He was cute and interesting. I flicked the receipt over in my hand and wondered how long I should wait to call him.

As I made my way through the forest path, which seemed much brighter and clearer to me now, I hummed to myself thinking about Darien's little tricks and white smile. At first, I was delighted, but the more I started to think, the more my heart started to drop.

What would he say if he found out I was an actual witch? When I was young, in my hometown, kids used to tease me and call me a monster and a freak and million other cruel names. Growing up with two moms was one thing, having those moms be the town witches was another thing entirely.

Parents used to give us sermons at the end of school functions and more than one kid told me that I was not allowed to come over to their house. They were afraid I was going to convert them to Satanism and lesbianism or both. Like I was some queer Darth Vader, trying to lure them over to the dark side.

As I got older, the kids stopped teasing me and just chose to ignore me which I preferred, since I could ignore them right back, and except for the occasional religious pamphlet, people stopped harassing us outright at the store. Well, at least people didn't graffiti it as much.

If Darien found out what I was, there was a good chance that he would never want to speak to me again. I mean, I almost burnt the receipt right in front of him. Magic tricks were all fun and games, but it's a whole other ball game when you have someone claiming to have actual powers. Especially, if there powers that you have no control over.

Even if he could accept me, I thought staring down at the receipt that was now crumbled in my fist. How could I know that I wouldn't hurt him? What if I ended up endangering him and I didn't even mean to?

The calls of girls brought my attention around from my thoughts as Tamara and Elaina ran up to me.

"There you are," yelled Tamara.

"We've been looking for you all day," Elaina finished.

"Sorry," I mumbled sheepishly, "I wanted to see what there was to do around here other than spells and schoolwork, so I took a little walk around the town. I must have lost track of time. I'm sorry if I worried anyone."

"It's okay," a soft voice purred behind me. I turned to see Mai standing cross-armed leaning against a tree, smirking, "I will admit, that we thought you might had tried to ditch the coven."

I laughed nervously and twirled a wave of hair around my finger, "No. I just needed a little me time."

"Are you alright from last night," Elaina whispered with concern, "I had never seen anyone pass out like that before. I thought you were having a seizure."

"What do you mean?" I asked. In nervousness, I ended up accidentally pulling the lock of hair that I was playing with. I bite back a yelp.

"Your eyes started rolling back and you were rocking and seizing and twitching all sorts of different ways," Tamara answered.

"Did I say anything?" Any excitement that I had from earlier in the day had no drained out of me and was now replaced with sheer fear and embarrassment.

"No," Tamara and Elaina said in unison.

"But you fell really hard," Tamara emphasized.

"Is this something that happens a lot," Mai asked intrigued, "because I've never seen someone pass out during a binding spell before."

"I…" I hesitated. What was I supposed to tell them. I didn't want them to think I was an absolute maniac.

"I had seizures a lot when I was younger," I lied, "They went away for a while, but now they've been starting to come back."

"Is it epilepsy?" Mai pressed.

"That doctors aren't sure what's wrong with me," I answered. The second part was not a complete lie. No one did now what was happening to me.

"I'm so sorry! Are you sure you're not hurt," Elaina questioned in her hushed tone.

"I swear. I'm fine," I answered, "It's just something that happens." Again, not a total lie.

Tamara patted me reassuringly on the shoulder and Elaina wrapped herself around me to give me a small hug.

It was a brief embrace, but I noticed a short quizzical glance she threw at me before Mai wrapped her arms around her shoulders.

"Sorry Mirah. We didn't know," Mai apologized, "Let's go get some dinner. We can help prep you for tomorrow," Mai added throwing a brilliant grin to me and the other girls.

There was a whoop and we began to make our way down to the main house as the sun started to sink behind the trees.

I breathed a sigh of relief. I had made a quick cover for now, but a nagging voice in the back of my head reminded me that I was playing a part and *no one can keep up a part forever.*

* * *

The next morning, I awoke early, my stomach churning with nerves. The night before, the girls had explained a normal day's schedule to me and what I would need to survive.

Supply wise, it was pretty simple on my part. Most items needed for spells and divination would be provided for us by the school, so it's not like I had to run out an pick up a magic wand or anything.

"Be on time." Tamara had told me, "They get absolutely livid when your late."

I would be more than on time. I thought checking my clock. The girls around me were still fast asleep. Mai was even gently snoring in the background.

After freshening myself up in the bathroom, I padded my way over to my wardrobe and took in my options.

"Black is a must," Mai had emphasized last night, "It's tradition. Also, no one looks bad in black, so it's a win win all around."

I pulled out a black pair of jeans and one of my favorite billowy, black blouses and readied myself to make my way to the main house, but before I left, I stopped and slunk back to the pants I wore yesterday, pulling the crumbled receipt out of my pocket.

The rest of the morning was peaceful, but stormy. The thunder rumbled gently in the background and fog swirled around your ankles when you walked.

I was starting to get to know more of the girls in the coven at breakfast, and my online classes were easy. But all I could think about was the afternoon. I wondered what we were going to learn and if I would make a fool out of myself.

After a quick lunch, which I barely touched, we made our way to the Sanctuary.

When we arrived, I noticed that, even though it was damp, instead of forming a circle like the girls had done previously, they sat neatly in rows on the grass facing the altar. The altar today contained multiple sets of new lightning rods and a couple of empty mason jars.

The rain started to increase and I shifted with discomfort in my wet seat. An older woman, with white, blonde hair, strode to the front of the altar and motioned her hands for us to rise.

"Welcome ladies! For those of you who don't know me, my name is Kalani and I will be your instructor for the day."

I saw a couple of eyes peek at me during Kalani's introduction, but otherwise, the girls gave their utter attention to the snow haired teacher. If the rain made any of them uncomfortable, none of them were showing it.

I brushed my damp hair off of my face and tried to ignore the grumble of thunder as it seemed to near our location. Kalani looked to the sky and calmly grabbed a lightning rod, balancing it gracefully on the tips of her fingers.

"Our focus today ladies, as many of you can guess, is storms. Storms are a great source of energy and use. The rain can be collected for spell and potion work," Kalani explained using the lighting rod to point to the mason jars that were slowly starting to fill.

"Storms themselves can be brought on through various spell work. There is magic as simple as whistling the wind, to as complicated as binding a storm to you."

The girls nodded with interest. I could see Mai out of the corner of my eye, had especially perked up and was staring at the lighting rod in Kalani's hand with great intensity.

"Magic during a rain storm is wonderful for purification and healing, but magic in a thunderstorm, such as today, well, that's when you can have a bit more fun."

"How so?" Mai called out. She looked like she could barely contain her excitement.

"Well, magic during a thunderstorm is great for communication. You can use the storm to send messages into the minds of people living far and wide. Some are even able to use the storm to communicate with the dead, as enough lighting can create enough energy to create spirit manifestation."

"How much lighting," Mai pressed.

"No small amount," Kalani intoned, "and using storms to speak to those who have passed away is no easy trick. There are very few who can do so, and those who can are mature, well-trained witches whose life focus has been storms.

Mai's shoulders dropped a hair, but even through the pouring rain, I could see the furrow of her brows and the determined line of her."

"So, what are we doing today?" Tamara called out from the back. There was tremble in her voice from shivering, and I had the feeling that she was not enjoying today's moist lesson either.

"I was just about to explain," Kalani answered. A smile curling into the corners of her mouth as she lifted her collar further up her neck. "As the jars fill for spells that we will performing throughout the week, we are going to be practicing some minor storm binding. Just so that I can see what level everyone is at and adjust my lessons to your needs."

"So," Kalani waved her rod in the air, "hopefully, some of you will be able to bind an entire storm to you after your training at the coven. But, for today, we are only going to focus on binding the lighting to us. We're not going to worry about the rain or the thunder. We are just going to focus on the lighting."

"Why the lighting?" Ariea questioned.

"Very good question," Kalani responded, "You see, lighting is a source of energy that is always looking to make a connection. Lighting needs to strike at some point. By manipulating the particles that make up lighting, you can ensure that it will want to connect with you, but without harm. Well at least no harm to you at least. You can use it to strike your enemies if you really want, but that is not what we are going to do today. Today, we will try and bind the lighting to us and then release back into the storm. If you are unable to bind the lighting today, no worries, I will adjust my lessons and you can work your way up, or maybe storm magic is just not your forte, which is fine.

"How does the spell work?" Mai pushed on, her eyes a glow in the fog.

"Patience Mai, I am getting to that," Kalani replied with a hint of annoyance.

"You see," Kalani lectured, "Some witches prefer to use wands to lure lighting to them. Some witches even get to the point where they can collect lighting in their hands. But, the easiest and most common way to connect to lighting is through a lightning rod.

The hairs on the back of my neck started to prickle. I had down a few spells and potions in the safety of my bedroom and kitchen, back at home, but I had never done anything as dangerous as trying to lure lighting to strike me.

It was interesting listening to Kalani teach, but I knew that there would be no way that I would be able to do this kind of magic. Behind me, there was a crack of lighting and my hands started to shake.

At best, they would discover that I was some sort of fraud. That I was a pathetic witch and they would drive me out of the coven. I would have to go back to my aunts with my head held down in shame. I would have to live my life being too strange for my normal peers, and not powerful enough for my coven sisters. I would be unaccepted in not just one, but two worlds.

Then, at worst, I could be struck by lighting and be terribly hurt or die. No matter what, it did not take a diviner to see that this little lesson was not going to end well for me.

"Now girls," Kalani instructed, "for this to work, you need to open up your mind and cleanse away any negativity from your mind."

Good luck with that, I thought as Kalani walked through the rows handing each girl a lightning rod.

"Now girls, I want you to just focus on my voice and the sounds of the storm. I will try and guide you through the binding process. Now close your eyes and take a deep breath."

I closed my eyes and tried to clear my mind, but the more I tried to relax, the more that my mind started to race. The only thing that kept popping into my head was that I was going to electrocute myself. I couldn't do this kind of magic. I was going to make a fool out of myself or end up in the emergency room.

"Control your thoughts," Kalani cried over the increasing sound of the wind and the pounding of rain, "In your mind I want you to picture a spark in the darkness. Nothing more. Just a small streak of light in the night."

I inhaled deeply, trying to ignore my worries and thoughts. It was kind of like meditating in yoga. In my head I first saw the darkness, that was easy to picture. Next, I thought of a tiny zap of light dancing all around like a lighting bug. I exhaled. Alright, this much I could handle.

"Now," Kalani boomed as thunder rolled around us, "I want you to imagine that spark starting to expand. Picture it growing upwards in the darkness."

I closed my eyes tighter and obeyed Kalani. As I meditated, I tried to ignore the chill in my bones from standing so long in the rain or the fact that I couldn't feel my toes any longer

"You see your lighting," Kalani instructed, "the next step, if you feel up to it, is to feel your lighting, I want you to imagine the static underneath your skin. I want you to hear the crackling in your ears, I want you…"

Kalani continued, but I could no longer hear her. The storm had begun to roar in full force. The rain pounded into our faces and the wind whipped around making it difficult to stand steadily. Part of me wanted nothing more than to go home and have a cup of coffee beside a roaring fireplace in my favorite bathrobe, but a deeper, more carnal part of me, refused to acknowledge the rain. This part of me wanted to prove myself. It wanted the power. It wanted the electricity.

In my mind, I could see the spark grow into lighting. The lighting spiraled upward into a whirling cloud hovering above the darkness. My entire body started to hum with energy. I could feel each particle of the storming growing into a crescendo. I held my breath. There was a eerie moment of dead silence, until Kalani's voice broke through my thoughts.

"Open your eyes," She shrieked.

I snapped open my eyes. Kalani continued to call to us like a general readying her troops to attack. "Hold your right hand up to the sky palm up."

Entranced, I raised my hand. Goosebumps rippled through my skin.

"Repeat after me," Kalani yelled, "*gilht ot em.*"

"*gilht ninb ot em,*" I answered.

"Good!" Kalani had to scream at the top of her lungs to be heard over the storm, "Now say *gilht erkits* and throw your hand down as hard as you can! Strike your lighting to the ground!"

I cried out the spell and, to my joy, I could feel the lighting hot charged in my hand. I was going to throw my palm down, when the thunder in my ears began to change.

It was lower, more guttural. I realized that it was not thunder I now heard, but laughter. A deep, baritone of a laugh egging me on. *Strike*! It laughed, *show them all what you can do.*

My hand stopped halfway down and I started to tremble. No. I thought. Whatever you are, I will not give you the satisfaction of having any control over me.

I could feel my hand start to singe from the unreleased heat, but I gritted my teeth and raised my hand back towards the sky. *Don't be a fool,* the voice purred, *release your power.*

"No!" I screamed. Then I heard new screams. No longer in my head, but coming from the girls around me.

"Mirah!," Kalani commanded, "through down your hand! You're hurting yourself!"

I could feel my hand grow hot. I could smell burnt skin and see smoke rising from the palm of my hand. It was agonizing, but I was frozen. I didn't know what to do. I tried calling out for help, but I couldn't speak. My knees shook and started to buckle and I wondered if I was going to pass out again, when I was forcefully tackled face first into the mud.

The spell was broken. The storm around us started to subside and the downpour was starting to become a sprinkle.

Groaning, I pushed myself up from the ground and tried to wipe the dirt from my face. As I clenched my palm, I felt a sudden rush of pain and I feel back to the ground writhing in pain.

The girls crowded around me, expressing their reassurances and concern. Tamara, who apparently was the one who power drove me into the ground kept apologizing again and again.

"Move over," Kalani ordered. Pushing girls out of her way, "Give her some room to breathe.

She softly touched my scorched palm, making me wince, "Mirah, why didn't you…" But before she could finish what she was about to say, Kalani let out a sharp gasp.

The other girls around me began to murmur with concern. Some drew away from me, while others inched closer to take a look at my hand.

I must have really burnt myself I thought, as I willed myself to look down and inspect the damage. When I looked down, I felt my breath leave my body, like I had been punched in the stomach.

My palm was hurt for sure, but it wasn't the burns that brought me so much fear. It was the shape the burns were formed into.

In the center of my palm was a charred upside-down pentacle. Even those who didn't practice witchcraft knew what this symbol meant. An upside-down pentacle was the mark of evil. The Dark Warlock had branded me.

CHAPTER TWELVE:

DARIEN

"You know, you never told me how I'm going to get this book out of me," I called out to Jude who was carefully wiping down a set of mirrors.

"When the time is right, the Book of Shadows will be summoned from within you," Jude responded curtly.

"How will I know the time is right? There is a lot of assuming going on here and you know what happens when you assume. You make an…"

"Just focus on getting the witch to trust you. She needs to trust you entirely for everything to work."

"Oh, I can get her to do more than just trust me," I responded with a wink. But then I thought of Mirah's serene face and the cool tinkle of her laugh. A small lump formed in my throat.

"I wouldn't be so confident," Jude snarked, "She still hasn't called you yet.

"What happens to Mirah when she signs the book," I asked Jude hesitantly.

"That sir, is none of your concern. You have one job. That is all you are responsible for," Jude snipped scratching at some chipped paint on a nearby table.

My throat got tighter. It was easy to agree to the deal when the other person didn't seem real. In my mind, she was just this imaginary witch all haggard and crooked nosed, but now that I knew that she was a real person, a likable person at that, everything seemed a lot more... complicated.

I shook my head. There was no use in getting attached. In the end, we all face the same inevitable fate. I knew what that fate could look like and I wanted to make sure that I ended up with the best ending possible.

"She'll call," I reassured Jude, "I mean, who could resist this," I laughed motioning up and down.

Jude rolled his eyes and continued to pace around the room, scratching and scrubbing at all sorts of different of different surfaces. I had never met someone who fidgeted as much Jude. It seemed like he could never sit still and it was starting to work on my nerves.

"For the love of God man, sit down. Watch you scurry around like that puts me on edge."

Jude sighed deeply again and sat down in the chair across from me. Even seated, he still could not settle down. His leg jiggled up and down and his fingers taped without rhythm on the table top.

I was tempted to yell at him. To order him to stop, but I realized that I knew nothing about this creature and how he had befallen such a fate. Who was he? What could he have possibly done to end up as the Dark Lord's lacky?

"So..." I drawled, "I guess if you're going to be my sidekick, we should get to know one another a bit."

"I am no sidekick," Jude snipped. His leg began to bounce more furiously making the table shake.

"How did you end up like this?" I pressed curiously, "How did you end up in the dark below?"

"That's none of your business," He barked, but I continued one with increasing curiosity.

"I mean your annoying," I added, ignore Jude's glare, "But you don't seem like that bad of a guy."

Jude exhaled so deeply that I wondered how one person could hold in that much air. He looked up at my with resentment. I thought he was going to ignore my question, but instead, he started to talk slowly, carefully choosing his words.

"I was always good with contracts and making… arrangements. I worked for an organization and helped them arrange payments for different people."

I stared blankly at him, "So, you were a banker?"

"Not exactly. The people I worked for were a bit more… underground."

I could feel my brow furrowed in confusion as I tried to figure out what on Earth he was talking about. Then it hit me like a pile of bricks.

"You were in the mafia?!" I yelped excitedly, inching closer.

"No need to yell," Jude responded waving me away.

"Was it like a Sopranos situation? Did you kill people?" I knew I was being rude, but I could not contain my curiosity.

"It was not as glamorous as what you see on TV. I promise you. Also, if we're being honest," Jude paused and started to pick at his nail nervously, "I did not kill anyone myself, but I lured people into deals I knew they couldn't keep. I kept the numbers and added the interest. I may not have shot the gun, but I was the one who signed their death certificate."

After this confession, I found that I had nothing to say. We sat for a couple minutes in an awkward silence, letting the minutes tick by. Suddenly, a sharp noise rang out through the theater startling Jude and I. We turned to the front office and heard the trill echo through the room again and again.

My heart leapt up to my throat. The sound was the ringing of the phone. I hurried to the phone, knowing that there would only be one person who would be calling. It was show time.

CHAPTER THIRTEEN:

MIRAH

After the storm lesson, Kalani brought me swiftly to a small house located on a short tree, that I was informed was the Medical House. The healer inside was a sweet, round faced plump woman who introduced herself as Flo. She smiled broadly at me at first and tutted over my burnt hand. But when I clenched my fist to show her the damage, her grin quickly disappeared.

She gave Kalani a look that I couldn't read and then began tending to my hand with laser focus. An earthy smelling balm was applied to my palm and my hand was neatly wrapped in record time. As Flo worked, I felt myself growing sleeping and wished desperately that I could go to bed. Not the emerald sheeted bed here, but my warm quilted bed at home.

Flo noticed my drooping eyelids and nodding head and urged me to lay back and rest for a while.

"With a little sleep, you'll be right as rain in no time," Flo chirped, but I noticed that her smile did not reach her worried eyes.

I had no energy left in me to protest. I slunk down into the soft sheets and wrapped my bandaged hand around the covers, pulling them up towards my neck.

"Good girl," Flo said patting my arm through the blanket, "I'll wake you up in an hour or so."

I nodded sleepily and felt myself begin to drift away. However, through the slits of my eyelashes, I could see Kalani and Flo whispering fervently to each other, throwing occasional nervous glances in my direction. I couldn't hear what they were saying. They were speaking softly and the need for sleep was pulling me down like an anchor.

I saw Kalani shake her head and turn to leave. She opened the door, turned to Flo and said the only fragment of their conversation that I could hear.

"She could be the death of us all."

I wanted to find out more, but I didn't have the energy. Before I could stop myself, I had fallen into a deep, dreamless slumber.

***

Flo woke me up some while later. Judging by the way the sun's rays were drifting below the trees, Flo had let me sleep for a lot longer than an hour.

I rubbed my sleep crusted eyes and winced as I clenched my wounded fist. I curled my hand open and closed, flexing my hand and testing my pain tolerance.

"That'll sting for a while dear," Flo explained to me. She sat down a steaming cup of sweet-smelling tea.

"They'll be a scar for a while," Flo continued, as I reached for the tea, "But hopefully, the balm I used on you should help it fade and in time it will disappear."

I thanked Flo for her healing and her tea. She brushed away my thanks and smiled at me sadly. I suddenly found myself longing to escape her pitiful gaze, so I forced myself to sit up in bed.

"Am I alright to leave," I questioned. I needed some time to be alone. I needed to process what was happening to mean and plan a course of action. Do I leave? Do I say? Should I tell my aunts? A frightening question slipped through my mind; would they even allow me to stay here? If they kick me out, where will I go? What is going to happen to me?

"You can head back to your room if you'd like, Flo reassured me, "I tried waking you up for dinner, but you weren't moving, so I let you rest a while longer. If you're hungry, I'm sure I can contact the kitchens and get something whipped up for you."

"That's alright," I smiled, "I'm not very hungry, honestly." It was the truth. I had no appetite at the moment. The only thing I wanted was to get away.

"Is there anything else you want me to look at? Is there anything at all bothering you physically or… mentally?"

"Nope!" I answered with fake cheer, "I feel right as rain. You're a life saver."

I swung myself out of bed and made my way to the door. The cool metal of the doorknob was a relief to my still burning palm and I was about to make my escape when I heard Flo call behind me.

"Mirah," Flo yelled. I turned to her expectantly.

"Protect yourself. Okay."

I nodded and threw and a throw away smile as I hustled my way out the door. I hurried to my room as Flo's word echoed through my head. *Protect yourself.* I wish I could, but how can one be protected from themselves.

* * *

I made my way to my house in the trees. In the sitting room Ariea was reading some thick book. She glanced up at me for a second, but then with disinterest, she returned to her reading. I suddenly felt arms wrap around me and felt myself lifted into the air.

"Mirah!" Tamara cried, "I'm so glad your Okay! You are Okay right? I'm sorry I pushed you to the ground, but I had to do something," Tamara was talking so fast her words started to jumble together. A couple of girls around us started to whisper, throwing dark looks in my direction as Tamara babbled her apologies.

"It's all good," I laughed throwing my hands up into the air.

"Oh, your poor hand," I mouse of a voice whispered at me. I turned to see Elania holding my hand with concern.

"It's nothing, really." I promised, "The healer gave me a balm and said I would be fit as a fiddle in no time."

"Mirah," Someone tapped me on the shoulder. I whipped around to see Mai, not looking at me with distaste or fear like the others, but with sincere interest, "What on Earth happened out there?"

"I… I don't know," I stammered.

"That burn on your hand was a symbol," Mai continued, "Do you know what that symbol stands for?"

I nodded, and to my horror, I felt tears start to well up in my eyes. Every witch had been taught about the Dark Warlock at some point. I remember my Aunt Lila telling me the story when I was young enough to still sit on her lap.

"The Dark Warlock. Some cultures have different names for him, but the idea is always the same. He was a Warlock from an age long ago who delved into the heart of dark magic." She had told me.

"He created spells that could turn a person inside out and remain alive. They said he could bring back the dead to do his bidding, and with a single word he could convince a person to leap of a cliff to their death. There was no dark spell that he did not know or could not master"

I had leaned forward, scared but fascinated. Lila pursed her lips, but had continued, "The legend has it that no amount of power was enough for him. That he took to seducing witches to sign his book. He would give them an infinite amount of magic, but in return they would sell their soul to him. With every soul collected, his power grew until his dark shadow crept around almost every corner of the world.

"Then one day he simply vanished, his army of soulless demons with him. Some naive witches believe that he gathered too much magic and that he ended up imploding on himself. However, wiser women believe that a coven of sorceress forced him away. Cast him into a dimension of fire and ash. Some people call this place hell, others call it the underworld, no matter what you call it, they say if you have a lost or cruel soul, he will snatch you away in your last breath of life and force you to live a life or servitude to him."

"But, he's gone, right?" I had asked wide eyed.

For once, Lila didn't smile, but instead looked at me with sad eyes, "I'm afraid, not my dear. I fear he still lingers on, biding his time."

"Biding his time for what?" I asked with a trembling lip.

Aunt Lila never answered me, but a voice deep in my gut told me what the Dark Warlock was biding his time for. He was waiting for me.

* * *

I shook the memory out of my head, refocusing back on the present. There was no point in trying to lie anymore. After passing out during the binding ceremony and the lighting incident, people already knew that I was a freak.

"I think there's something wrong with me," I whimpered.

"Hey. Hey. Don't cry," Mai whispered. Mai grabbed my arm and started to usher me up the stairs, motioning for Tamara and Elaina to follow.

"Whatever is going on, we will help you through it," Elaina murmured.

"No. It's fine," I tried to argue, but Mai interrupted me.

"Listen. As of the other night, we are bound as sisters now. If something is wrong, we're going to help you. Don't even bother arguing."

The tears that I had been trying to hold back slipped down my cheeks and I unleashed a small sob. I had only known these girls for a short amount of time, but the kindness they were showing me was more than I deserved.

Tamara rubbed my shoulder in comfort, as Mai charged into the bedroom. "Now, sit down and…" Mai's order was cut off but a short gasp. I heard a yelp from Elaina behind me and Tamara leapt in front of me to try and block my view.

"What's going on?" I demanded, pushing Tamara aside. Then I saw what the girls were trying to hide.

My bed had been brutally slashed. Sage was burnt out into my sheets like cigarettes in an ashtray and candle wax was smeared all over her sheets and bedside table. Above my bed, in bold, dark letters was the message "BEGONE DEMON FREAK!" The paint was still fresh and dripped onto my pillow in small black puddles.

"Those bitches," Tamara yelled, "We're going to find out who did this Mirah. I'll slap it out of them if I have to."

I'll clean up your bed and get you some new sheets," Elaina cried, hustling to the bathroom to try and get some towels.

"Mirah don't listen to those girls," Mai began, but I wasn't listening. I had been made fun of before, but never to this extent. I was wrong to think that I could belong here. Whoever wrote this was right. I am a demon monster.

I felt new tears start to spring to my eyes. *No,* I thought. I will not anyone else the satisfaction of seeing me cry. I turned my heel, breaking out of Mai's grasp and sprinted out the door. As I passed through the common room, I heard faint giggling and the whispers of *freak* as I ran out the door.

I ran as far as I could away from that house until I ran out of breath. I collapsed against and nearby tree and tried to think of my options.

I couldn't call my aunts. I couldn't bear to let them know what a failure I had become. I certainly was not going to go back to that freaking treehouse. At least not yet, not if I had any choice.

But where could I go? I only had about forty dollars of my own money on me. My aunts had given me a debit card in case of emergencies, but if I started using that they were going to start asking questions sooner than later.

I was stuck. I had nothing and no one. I was branded and alone. I put my head in my hands and unleashed a primal scream into the night. My throat was sore, but I screamed again and again, enjoying the release of my pent-up rage and fear.

When my throat was raw, I slumped further against the tree, trying to catch my breath. Suddenly, a desperate idea struck me and I dove my hand into my pocket. I pulled out the crumpled receipt with Darien's number from yesterday and stared at it. I really didn't know anything about this guy. I was dirty and hurt and not exactly in any sort of shape for a date. Also, I doubt he would be cool with the idea of some random stranger crashing at his place, but if I could convince him to let me come over just for a couple hours, it could help me take my mind of things and maybe help me think of a better plan, or at least collect myself before I had to face those girls again. I didn't want to give them the satisfaction of me running away, but I needed to prepare to see them again.

It was the only option I had. Determined, I crept towards the Main Hall, which to my relief, was empty. I wandered down the halls until I found a series of tiny rooms with the sign "Phones" above them.

Beneath them, was the rules for phone etiquette which included keeping one's calls to no longer than an hour, keeping a respectable volume, and avoiding "intimate" conversations.

I dove into the nearest room. The phone was hilariously old fashioned and I couldn't help but laugh aloud. It must have been white once, but time had turned it into more of a murky tan. I even had a rotary dial, which took me a while to figure out how to decipher.

After I got the phone to work, I clutched the earpiece tight against me. My eyes closed in desperation. I didn't know what my next step was going to be if Darien didn't answer.

Finally, the ringing stopped followed by a split second of silence. My heart pounded in anticipation. Then I heard the three words I had been praying for purr into my ear.

"Hello, Darien Burron."

CHAPTER FOURTEEN:

DARIEN

I hung up the phone and threw a celebratory smile at Jude. Mirah had called and half begged to see me. It looks like death had not taken away my boyish charm. I hurried around trying to think of what to do and where to take Mirah.

After a bit of pacing, I forced myself to calm down. I'll just ask her what she wants to do, she did call me in the first place. I shooed Jude for privacy and freshened up, all while trying to ignore the twinge of guilt that crept in the corners of my mind.

I shook my head. There was no use in feeling sorry. I barely knew this girl and in order to survive, sometimes sacrifices have to be made. Hell, I didn't even know why the Dark Lord wanted her so much, maybe she was secretly a horrible person and I was doing the world a favor.

There was a knock at the theater door and I ran over to open it. Steeling myself and forcing a winning, I swung open the door and prayed that Jude and I had cleaned the place enough that she would be impressed rather than repulsed.

Mirah stepped in looking bedraggled and tired. Her clothes were sagging like she had slept in them and she had a dirty bandage around her right hand. This wasn't a date, I realized. It was an escape plan.

I swallowed back a groan of frustration and instead welcomed Mirah in the lobby. She sat wearily on one of the plush red chairs and drank the water that I offered her in one gulp. I started awkwardly trying to think of what to say and what to do.

When she had finished her drink, she looked around the theater curiously. Her cool, dark eyes made me self-conscious as they roamed around and I found myself trying to make excuses in order to impress her.

"Sorry for the mess," I stammered to my chagrin, "We have been doing some remodeling and the…"

"I love it," Mirah interrupted, breaking into a wide smile, "It's cozy and it reminds me of a different time."

I found myself smiling back with relief and I offered my arm to her to give her a tour. As I showed her the dressing room and costumes, I noticed she laughed and leaned against me, but it was more for support than any kind of flirtation.

I only showed her a few rooms on out little "tour" because I was afraid of running into Jude and also because I was desperate to find some way to move things forward. The book pressed against me from the inside of my chest with each breath like the ticking of a clock.

"So," I smirked, "We don't need to stay in this stuffy theater all night. What would you like to do? Movies? Dinner? An elaborate diamond heist?"

"As tempting as those all sound, especially the last one," She replied, "I'm actually fine with just hanging out here for a little bit, maybe just getting to know each other."

She sunk into a nearby chair and I felt my smile falter for just a second, before I swallowed and straightened my posture. No problem. I didn't need extravagant dates to be charming.

"Well in that case," I replied sitting next to her, "If you want to stay in my theater then your going to have to give me something in return."

She looked at me cautiously, and I held out my hands in innocence, "Show me some of that magic you were talking about the other day. I showed you a trick. You still owe me."

She laughed and I saw her visibly relaxed as she sunk deeper into the seat. I watched her think for a moment and then she grabbed my hand.

"Alright mister," She smiled, "How about a palm reading."

"By all means," I answered holding my arm further out to her.

Despite her cold eyes, her hands were warm and almost burned at the touch. She trailed the index finger across the palm of my hand, making me shiver involuntarily.

"What would you like me to start with?" She questioned, "Love? Fortune? Life?"

"Oh, fortune please. If I'm going to die early, it would be nice to know if I live a life of riches before I kick the bucket."

She rang her finger across the line starting between my middle and ring finger and traced it down my palm.

"This is your fate line," Mirah explained, "This shows what affect you will have on the world. This could mean money, but it could also mean fame or just general influence."

"Fancy. So, tell me, Madam Mirah, am I destined for fame and fortune?"

"Madam Mirah, I like that," She laughed and then continued, "Your fate line is not just one single line, but broken into a few short lines. That usually indicates a sudden change, a different career, an interruption towards one's life, or a general change of fate itself."

"So… My life is going to change and I suddenly going to become a handsome billionaire," I asked raising an eyebrow.

"Hard to say," Mirah giggled, "But it looks like you won't be in the magic business forever, or at least in the position you are now. Which by the way, what exactly do you do here? Where is everyone else?"

"I own this theater. I'm the main magician, so it's really just me. I have an... assistant that helps clean on occasion, but I'm pretty much the only one running the show." It wasn't a complete lie. The theater was mine now and I even thought of trying to start the shows up again to try and make some extra money.

"Wow, that's amazing," Mirah gasped, "How did this happen? How were you able to afford this?"

"I thought I was the one that was supposed to be asking the questions here," I replied carefully trying to dodge Mirah's questions, "Tell me about my love life now. Is true love waiting just in front of me?" I flirted.

Mirah blushed and it looked like I had successful distracted her from her previous inquiries and she scanned over my open hand.

"See here," Mirah said her fingers tickled the top of my hand and I felt myself enjoying the feel of her touch, "This is your Heart Line it can show you the emotional state of a person as a whole, which can then reflect on how they act in romantic relationships."

"What does mine say?" I asked inching closer to her face.

"Yours is very interesting. It starts and ends high. That means you are a rather emotional and impulsive person."

I wouldn't say I'm terribly emotional, but I must that I am prone to impulse," I chuckled.

Mirah grinned and continued, "According to your heart line, you don't have the best self-control and are quite outgoing. But the line is concave, which suggests there is a hidden sensitivity to you. As a partner, you'd be a lot to deal with and a constant adventure, but you would also care about your partner and their feelings."

"I see. I'm obnoxious, but I care. Seems pretty accurate," I snarked.

Mirah laughed loudly, "Pretty much."

"Does that sound like someone you would be interested in," I pressed.

"I'm sure some girls would be," Mirah answered mysteriously. I tried to read her face for any hint of emotion, but her expression was as neutral as still water.

"Alright, Mistress Mirah," I joked, "Time for the grand finale. Tell me how it all ends for me. Shall I go down in a blaze of glory."

I was trying to keep my tone light, but at the idea of death, I thought back to those harsh lights, the agonized cries of my friends, and the endless tedium of purgatory. I had a sudden urge to wrench my hand away from her, but I forced myself to hold it steady.

She glided her finger down the line between my index finger and thumb. Her touch was so gentle it almost tickled and I found myself having to grit my teeth to keep from laughing.

She kept retracing the line and I watched her eyebrows slightly furrow. When she begins speaking again, her words are slow and deliberate, like she's trying to tread carefully on what she's trying to say.

"There are a couple of breaks in your life line. Now that can mean that there may be some serious accidents of illnesses in your future, but," she looks up me thoughtfully, "it could also mean that you will be having some serious changes in your future."

"That's not very specific," I joke.

"Palm reading is not an exact science. It is unique to every individual and is meant to be taken as more of a guideline to one's life then an actual life plan. The palm can you show you what you can be, but in the end we are always in charge of our own fate."

"That's deep," I grin, but something about her little speech affected me. I could feel my breath slow and my shoulders droop from a tension I didn't even know that I had. Talking with Mirah was like curling up in a favorite blanket, soothing and easy.

Mirah didn't answer. She just released my hand gently. I couldn't help examining my palm. I stared over the groves and marks trying to find to understand what hidden meanings she had found within the lines.

"Where did you learn to read palms?" I asked breaking the silence.

"My Aunt Gerta taught me," She explained, smiling wistfully at a memory, "She owns a small Pagan store and sometimes we would offer palm and tarot readings to try and earn a bit more money.

"You come from a line of witches?" I inquired, "What about your parents, if you don't mind me asking.

"No idea. My mother died right after I was born and I never met my father. My aunts were the ones who raised me," Mirah replied. There was an awkward silence until Mirah sprung up lightly from her chair and started to pace around.

"I can't thank you enough for letting me come over," she called over her shoulder.

"It really is no problem. You can stay as long as you'd like," I replied meaning every word, "You sounded like you were in a bit of a tight spot."

She grimaced and I cringed hoping that I hadn't said the wrong thing.

"All I'm saying is that my schoolmates can be… a lot. But," She throws a wide grin at me, "I feel a lot better now thanks to you."

"I'm at your service," I answered with a mock bow.

"I do have to go back eventually," She sighs, "People are probably looking for me and I also don't want to give those girls the satisfaction of feeling like they had run me out."

I was tempted to ask what the girls had done that was so bad, but from my past experience with women, I found it was better not to involves one's self in female drama.

"Well I'd like to see you again, but under happier circumstances," I suggest.

"Me too," She agrees, "Maybe we can see that movie you were talking about or maybe you can get me some tickets to your show."

"Absolutely," I reply as an idea starts to take form in my brain.

Mirah says her farewells and she's just about to exit the door when I leap up and grab her wrist.

"Hey Mirah, do you want some extra money and have the chance to hang out." The words slip out of me. It's the perfect plan. Maybe not completely thought out, but I could make it happen.

"Sure," She ventures warily, "What do you have in mind?"

"Work with me. You could be my magician's assistant in the magic show. I don't have one and with my tricks and your natural gifts, we could be a shown like no one has ever seen before. Besides, it always helps the magician keep the audience distracted when there's a pretty girl on the stage."

There's soft color to her cheeks and her eyebrows knit together in a now familiar expression.

"So," I press. "What it'll be?"

CHAPTER FIFTEEN:

MIRAH

I arrived back to the Sanctuary late that night. The long walk to get to Darien's theater had been a great way to clear my head, but I was to make the long trek again so late at night.

I had gotten a cab to bring to as close as the woods as they would take me. The taxi driver was extremely confused as to why a young girl would want to be dropped off in front of the woods in the middle of the night, but he got me to where I needed to me.

As I walked, I checked my wallet. The fare had used up a good chunk of what cash I had. The walk back was slow and precarious as I found myself tripping over unseen roots, but it gave me the time to puzzle over Darien's proposal.

Some extra cash my way certainly wouldn't hurt and it also would be nice that I had something to turn to if the coven decided to toss me out on my rear in the morning. As for Darien, himself, I was drawn to him that was for sure. But there was something about him, something that I couldn't place that seemed off. It was like looking into a two-way mirror.

I got to the Sanctuary and was relieved to see that it appeared quite silent and empty. Hopefully, everyone had gone to sleep and I would be able to slip in without much attention.

Where would I sleep? I thought of my ruined bed as I crept my way across the long, wet grass. When I arrived at the Green House I peered through the door at the common room. The room was completely dark except for the last embers of fire that were starting to burn out in the fireplace.

With each step I tip toed up, I psyched myself with what I was going to say and do when I got into the bedroom. I'd kick one of those girls out of their bed if I have to, I told myself. I'll keep them all awake until I get some new sheets. I would make sure that they never tried to mess with me again.

I swung open the door and prepared for battle, but instead was greeted with a rush of dark hair and strong arms as Tamara lifted me off the ground in a bear hug and Mai and Elaina babbled over each other.

"Oh my God, Mirah where were you?" We were getting so worried," Elaina asked in her usual soft tone.

"When you left, we marched over to Martha's house and demanded to see her. She was furious when she found out what had happened," Mai explained.

"She came back here and screamed at the girls. Demanding to know who did it," Tamara continued releasing me from her grasp.

"I'd never seen Martha so mad," Elaina murmured fervently.

"Did anyone confess?" I asked startled.

"No. Cowards," Mai snarled glaring around the room. No one would meet her eyes.

"But between the rage of Mai, Tamara, and Martha, I don't think anyone is going to bother you again," Elaina chirped quietly.

"You guys didn't have to do that," I whispered touched.

"Of course, we did," Mai insisted, "You're our friend. Besides, no one should be treated that way. Period."

My heart ached at their kindness and I found myself at a loss for words. I nodded gratefully and walked over to my bed. The mattress and the sheets had been replaced with fresh linen. I could also see that someone had obviously attempted to wipe away the message over my bed. The words were smeared and faded, but the message was still clear. They may try and hide their feelings, but someone still didn't want me here.

I peered around the dimly lit bedroom. Most of the girls were trying to get back to sleep after Mai and Tamara's exclamations, but in the gloom, I could feel eyes slide across me from under eyelids and out of the corners of eyes. I was being watched, that's for sure. There was no way I was going to let my guard down anytime soon.

* * *

The next morning, I was trying to eat my breakfast without incident when I felt a sharp tap on my shoulder. I looked up to see Ariea looking terribly tired and bored.

"Martha wants to see you in her quarters," Aria droned looking like she'd rather be talking to anyone else but me.

"I don't know where…"

"I've been instructed to show you," Ariea interrupted rolling her eyes.

I gulped down what was left of my toast, threw a curious glance at Mai who gave me a shrug, and followed Aria out of the dining hall.

It was a beautiful, sunny morning and the grass was covered in dew as we made our way across the grounds. Martha's house was located further back in the Sanctuary nestled in the shadows under the branches of a patch of tall, twisting trees.

Ariea strutted purposefully to the front door and gave it a sharp knock. She then turned swiftly on her heel and walked away without looking back or saying another word.

The door opened and I heard Martha's voice call to me from within. I hesitantly walked into the house wondering what Martha could have wanted from me at this point. Was she mad at me for leaving yesterday? Did she want to apologize for the girls? I wasn't sure, but my thoughts were soon distracted by the tranquil beauty that was Martha's living space.

The room was dimly lit by those small orbs that I had grown to become accustomed to and the walls were a light gray tinged with decorative elements of golden leaves. Along the walls were stunning oil painting of fairy folk. Everything was as pristine as a museum, and the whole area was filled with the rich smell of oak and earth.

Seated at a twisting, golden desk was Martha who was in a quiet conversation with Kalani who was standing on her right side. To her left was a woman I didn't recognize. She was could not have been older than forty, but she appeared to be very frail and delicate. Everything from her thin hands to the thin strands, of blonde made this woman look as if she would break if she was handled too roughly.

"Mirah, Come on in. Please, take a seat." Martha motioned to a small, golden stool in front of the desk.

I perched on the end of the stool, trying to gird myself up for whatever was going to be said and to prepare myself to be able to make a quick getaway if I needed to.

"First of all," Martha began, "I want to apologize on the behalf of the coven for the incident with you bed yesterday. That sort of behavior is not acceptable here and I want you to know that we are doing everything we can to try and apprehend whoever vandalized your things."

"It's really no big deal," I explained embarrassed.

"No, Mirah, it is a big deal," Kalani interrupted.

"In this coven, we need to be able to trust one another. If we turn on one another, then who is to stop the world from turning on us. The world in the past has not been kind to witches. We must always strive to protect one another. Protect the coven or watch it burn. That is still the way our world works. So, by attacking you, those girls were attacking our coven and we will not stand for that. So, Mirah, please promise me that if anything happens to you again, you will let one of us know. Okay?

I nodded and inched forward on the stool preparing to leave, but then I felt a feeble hand on my shoulder pushing me back down.

"Before you leave, there are some questions we want to ask you Mirah," Kalani explained in a clipped tone.

I looked around bewildered as the three women looked knowingly at one another.

"Mirah," Martha started slowly, "Can you explain what happened the other day at the storm lesson? Kalani told me that you were doing a wonderful job at binding the storm at first, by then something went… awry. What was the issue?"

How much of the truth should I tell them? I thought to myself. On one hand, I wanted answers to what was happening to me, but on the other hand, a part of me was hesitant to let these women in. What if they turned on me like everyone else?

Well," I began trying to choose my words carefully, "I was following Kalani's instructions and focusing on a spark. It was growing and I could feel my energy growing with it, but then when it when it was time to throw the lighting down," I hesitated. I could feel their eyes piercing through me, listening, waiting, "I couldn't," I finished lamely.

"Why not," Martha pressed. The strange, frail woman beside her latched onto my eyes with a piercing stare. Her green eyes bore into mine and I felt my body start to tremble and sweat began to form on my upper lip.

"I. I just couldn't. I couldn't let go," I answered. My voice shook and I felt a tug on my chest.

"Why couldn't you let go Martha," barked, "What was holding you back?"

"I don't know," I stammered. My entire body started to vibrate and my hand started to burn.

"Tell us the truth Mirah. No harm will come to you," Martha promised.

The tug on my chest tightened and I could feel words come unbidden to my lips. I tried to swallow them back down. But my throat was too tight and the words tumbled out of me before I could stop them.

"There was a voice in my head," I whispered trembling, "It kept telling me to strike the lighting. To show my power, but I didn't want to do what the voice said. I knew that if I listened to that voice something bad would happen."

"This voice," Martha asked leaning forward across her desk know, "Was this your voice or someone else's? Was it someone you recognized?"

"No," I replied. The sweat was pouring down my face and I felt myself gasping for air, "I've heard this voice before, but I don't know who it belongs to."

"You've heard this voice before," Martha questioned, "Where?"

"Back home a few times. I don't like the voice. I don't trust it. It wants to hurt people. But I don't, I swear. I would never hurt anyone. That's why I wouldn't let the lighting go. I wouldn't listen to him and he hurt me." I reached my arm forward to emphasize my point.

Suddenly, it was the like the threads pulling on my chest were snapped. I fell backwards in the stool, clutching my chest trying to control my breath. As I wheezed, I saw Martha nod towards the strange woman on her left.

"Thank you, Claire. You may go now." Without another word the delicate blonde wiped her brow and left the room. I found myself more angry and confused than ever before.

"What did she do to me!" I cried angrily.

"I'm sorry Mirah," Martha apologized, "but for the safety of the coven we needed to get some answers and we needed to make sure that you were being truthful. Claire's is an extremely talented clairvoyant. She can not only read minds when she wants to, but she can get people to speak their minds despite themselves. It's very difficult magic for all parties involved and it takes a lot out of Claire, but as I mentioned before Mirah, we needed so honest answers from you."

"What were these answers you were so concerned about," I snarled feeling betrayed. I did not appreciate having someone control my mind without my consent.

"The burn on your hand is concerning," Kalani explained softly, "It's not just some random burn mark, it's the sign of…"

"I know what it's a sign of," I cry frustrated, "and if you want the truth so bad, I can tell you that it doesn't mean anything. I am not some darkness worshipper if that is what you are afraid of."

"We don't think you worship the darkness," Kalani soothed, "In fact we're trying to protect you."

"By ganging up on me and messing with my mind," I screamed, "That's a funny way to try and protect someone."

"We're worried that the Dark Warlock is trying to ensnare you," Martha's blunt response struck across me like a slap.

"Me? What on Earth would the Dark Warlock want with me?"

"We're not sure," Martha explained, "But that's why we need to get to the bottom of things as soon as possible."

"Have you or your family had any experience with dark magic," Kalani pried.

"No!" I screamed. Standing up and starting to storm out. It was one thing for people to question me, it was a whole other experience to have people suggesting that my family were some kind of monsters.

"Mirah please wait!" Kalani yelled out to me, "I didn't mean any offense. We're just trying to understand what's going on."

"What's going on with me is none of your concern and if your so worried about me hurting your precious, little coven, then throw me out and be done with it!"

"That's not what we want," Martha sighed, "We want to help you."

"How on Earth do you think you can help me?" I snarled. I was normally a fairly taciturn person, but something about the way these women were looking at my cautious with a tinge of pity, made me feel like a feral animal trapped in a corner.

"If there is some dark force trying to possess you, we can try to exorcise it out," Kalani called out to me.

I hesitated; it was true that there was something wrong with me. That could not be denied. Didn't I want the answers to what was happening to me? If I took these women up on their offer, did I really have anything to lose?

"What would an exorcism entail?" I asked nervously. Images of waving crosses and rotating heads flickered across my mind.

"It would be a small, private ceremony," Martha reassured me, "No theatrics, just some herbs and spells to cleanse the spirit. But for us to perform the ceremony properly Mirah you have to tell us what has been going on with you. We need all the details if we are supposed to help you."

I swallowed. I could turn around, tell them that their being crazy, but as I looked down at my searing hand, I knew that I could not continue living like this. I needed answers and this may be the best option I have.

I turned to Martha and sighed deeply, "Let me start from the beginning."

Chapter Sixteen:

Darien

I'm telling you Jude; the cape works wonders on you."

I was temporarily blinded as Jude threw a bejeweled cape in my face, blocking my vision. We had been working furiously to try and get the theater in running shape, which was no easy feat for two people, even if one was a demon deal-maker.

"Why are we spending so much time on this ridiculous theater," Jude snapped, "We should be focusing on the getting the girl to sign the master's book."

"That is exactly what I'm doing," I answered twirling an old-fashioned black and white magic wand between my fingers, "This theater is the key to getting Mirah on our side. If she agrees to work with us, then we'll be spending a lot of time together, and then," I slide the tip of the magic wand down so that it became a bouquet of fake flowers and handed them to Jude, "I will make her mine."

"You mean you will make her master's," Jude replied smacking the flowers out of my hand.

"Same difference," I called. My chest tightened at the thought, but I brushed it aside as I dove further into the prop closet. Restoring the theater had become an obsession of mine since Mirah had left the other night. I couldn't place why, but something inside of me knew that getting this show together would be the key to seeing Mirah again.

I stared down at my palm and glided my finger across my palm lines. I wanted to see Mirah again, and if I was being honest with myself, I didn't just want to see her again because of the deal.

I clenched my fist and shook my head. I couldn't afford to think this way. There was work to be done and I was going to ensure that when I was back in the afterlife, I was going to have a sweet deal waiting for me.

"If you really want to make yourself useful," I chirped at Jude who was fidgeting around with a set of trick top hats, why don't you go and hand out some flyers. With your sweet smile and warm demeanor, I'm sure you'll have people flocking to our theater in no time."

Jude rolled his eyes at me, grabbed a stack of flyers that I had printed out earlier, and stalked out of the room.

Once he had left, I let out a sigh of relief. Working with Jude was like working with a very organized toy soldier. He was constantly being wound up and whirled around the space in a stiff nervous fashion and it was starting to get to me.

I walked over the trick top hats that Jude was adjusting and flipped one onto my head, chuckling nervously to myself. All of this relied on Mirah agreeing to work with me. If she didn't agree to work at the theater, or worse, if I never heard from her again. All of this work would be for nothing. I didn't have her number; I didn't know where she lived. There was no Plan B. She had to call.

I took off the hat and pushed open the top. This was so that the magician could reach his arm through and pull a rabbit or flowers out of the hat. It was an old trick, but still a favorite amongst audiences. I wondered if I should pick up a rabbit before the show.

I worked on, ignoring the fear and doubt that tickled the me in the back of my mind. She was going to call. She had to.

She didn't call that night, or the next. By the third night, I was about to give up hope when I was surprised, by the ringing of the phone, but by the knock of a door.

CHAPTER SEVENTEEN:

MIRAH

I told Martha and Kalani everything. I told them about the dark voices in my head and how it urged me to do terrible things. I told them about the incident in my aunt's store and how that was the catalyst for them sending me away. I told them how I was afraid of finally losing control and hurting someone.

They listened to everything in an attentive silence. When I was finished, I found that I was quite exhausted. I sunk deep into the stool and put my head in my hands.

"You are very brave for telling us all of this," Kalani said rubbing my shoulder.

"We're going to try and do what we can to help you Mirah. You're one of us now. I'm sorry you have to go through this," Martha murmured.

"What do you think is wrong with me," I whispered. My heart raced, but I needed to know what they were going to say.

Martha sighed and threw Kalani a concerned glance, "Unfortunately Mirah this is what we feared would happen. I'm going to tell you straight because I think you can handle it,"

She paused as I gaped at her, clinging to every word she said.

"I think you're a nice girl and I think you could be a very talented witch with the right amount of training. But there is a dark force within you. I felt it from the moment I saw you. As long as that dark force is present you will never be able to live a full life. You will constantly be two halves trying to battle their way for dominance and that is no way to live."

"So, what am I going to do," I asked feeling defeated.

"We are going to exorcise this darkness from you," Martha retorted, "It's not going to be easy. Even in the best circumstances, it takes a lot of energy on all parties involved and this ceremony has not been performed in the Sanctuary for many years, but we are going to do everything we can to help you."

I nodded, but one question still lingered in my mind. It was the question that haunted me more than any of the others.

"Why me," I insisted, "Why is this happening to me?"

"I wish I knew Mirah. I really do," Martha sighed sadly, "In life, sometimes we get thrown mountains for no rhyme or reason. All you can do is lift your chin and try and climb over it."

"But you don't have to climb alone Mirah," Kalani added.

"No, you don't," Martha reassured me, "Go to your classes like normal today. Then tonight at three in the morning, come down to the Sanctuary. We will try our best to help rid you of these troubles."

I gave a single nod and rose up from the stool, my legs felt wobbly and unsteady as I made my way to the door.

"Take it easy today Mirah. Don't push yourself to hard in your lessons and have a good dinner," Kalani called out to me, "You are going to need your strength for the ceremony to work."

I promised her and tried to throw her a relaxed smile, but the muscles in my lips were frozen.

"Oh, Mirah," Martha added, "One last thing before you go." I turned and looked at her curiously. "Don't tell the other girls about tonight. It's a private spell and the other students would just interfere. Do you understand?"

"Yes," I choked out and with a wave of approval, Martha motioned me to the door.

I stumbled out of the entrance blinded by the sudden shine of the sun. I tripped my way over to a patch of grass and laid down, letting my eyes adjust to the new light. I soaked in the sun hungrily. Even though I could hear the happy cries of the girls far behind me, I found that I couldn't bring myself to draw away from this little peace. It was comfortable and warm, but even more so, a frightened voice in my mind kept urging me to savor this moment. Savor this time because there was a chance that I might never see the sunlight again.

* * *

The rest of the day passed in a blur. I told my friends that Martha just wanted to talk about the dorm incident from last night. Then I clicked through my normal online classes without thinking and the magic lesson was a calm study of different kinds of medicinal herbs that had many of the girls yawning.

I couldn't stop wondering what was going to happen to me. I mean when I heard the word "exorcise" I pictured images of floating girls with rotating heads vomiting around the room. Was that what was going to happen to me? Was this ceremony going to hurt? What if it didn't work and I just got worse. The questions raced through my mind, but one question echoed over the others, Why me?

I was no one special. I certainly never dabbled in dark arts or messed with some sorceress who could have cursed me. Out of all the girls in the world, why did I have to be the one that was possessed by some dark force.

I couldn't stop thinking about it. At dinner, despite Kalani's urgings to eat a large dinner, I found that I could barely choke a spoonful down. The chatter of the girls around me was just white noise as I lost myself in my own thoughts. I tried thinking of every possible explanation, every logical conclusion as to why this was all happening to me, but I couldn't think of a single reason. Maybe it was just my fate to have horrendous luck.

Though the day went quickly, the night ticked by with agonizing slowness. I watched the minutes creep by and as each girl slowly started to grow drowsy and turn into their beds for the night, I was filled with a restless energy that I couldn't contain.

Trying to read or do any homework was a lost cause. I could not concentrate long enough to hold any sort of real conversation. Instead I spent the night jiggling my leg and staring at the imposing Grandfather clock that swung ominously in the corner of the common area.

After what felt like eons, it was almost time. I sprang carefully as to not wake the other girls, out of the house and slunk my way to the Sanctuary as my heart beat loudly in my chest.

I arrived at the Sanctuary and saw a few older women standing clustered in a group. I recognized Martha in the center of the group from her red, spiraling hair, but all the others had their hoods up and were unrecognizable to me.

I could run away. I considered. No one is making me go through this. I could go back and say that I feel asleep and lost track of the time. I could sprint through the trees to the nearest clearing and take Darien up on his offer to work in his magic show. Then I would never have to worry about these women again. But, as much as I wanted to get away, a bigger part of me wanted my freedom back. I wanted to be able to perform magic without fear of repercussions. I wanted to feel in control of my own body and mind again. I wanted to be me again.

After a deep breath, I strode out into the center of the clearing. A bat fluttered over ahead and I didn't need a clock to know what time it was. It was three o'clock in the morning. The witching hour.

Martha greeted me and lead me by the hand to the altar that had held the lightning rods from the class a few days ago. Now the altar was cleared, and Martha bade for me to lay down on it.

Nervously, I laid down, shivering at the cool touch of the stone. Other than a few reassurance and instructions from Martha, no one else in the Sanctuary spoke a word. I was starting to wonder if I had made a terrible mistake and if it was too late to try and form some plan of escape.

"Mirah," Martha whispered solemnly to me. I felt my body shake and I knew it wasn't just from the cold.

"I need you to listen to me carefully," Martha instructed, "This is not an easy ceremony to perform and the smallest mistake could have very serious consequences."

I nodded, but I felt my breath hitch. No one said anything about consequences.

"There's nothing you have to do Mirah," Martha promised me and a calming tone, "You just need to listen and breathe. Don't hold your breath as you may pass out and then we will have to stop the ritual, but other than that, we will take care of the work."

I nodded again more vigorously then I meant to. I could breathe. That was one of the few things I felt I could do confidently.

"This may become uncomfortable, maybe even a bit painful," Martha warned, "But, remember to just keep breathing."

I didn't even nod. I just felt my eyes dart around in pure panic. What did she mean by painful? What was going to happen to me?

But before, I could make a run for it, Martha's voice boomed through the still night air.

"Ladies, it's time."

Suddenly all of the candles and orbs surrounding the Sanctuary were extinguished except for one, long, flickering, black candle held in Martha's hands.

The women circled around me, making me feel very much like a cornered animal. I had no way to escape now.

Softly, I heard Martha begin to chant in a language that I didn't understand. Soon, the other women in the circle began to join her, their voices growing louder with each incantation.

My shivering increased, but I was not growing colder. Sweat began to drip down my forehead and I found myself pulsing to the rhythm of their spell.

Martha lifted her hands into the air and stared into the sky screaming. Even if I could understand her, I wouldn't have been able to known what she was saying as a roar rushed to my ears deafening me.

I wanted to call out to them. I was desperate to know when this would end, but when I opened my mouth, I found my voice had left me. All I could form was a silent scream into the darkness.

Martha reached into the inside of her robe and pulled out a dagger. It was longer and more curved than the one used in the binding ceremony and as she raised it to the sky my very veins began to boil. It was agony writhing around on that forsaken stone slab and with each passing moment, I knew that I had made a terrible mistake coming here tonight.

Suddenly, the chanting stopped. The silence was deafening and I knew that we were reaching the crescendo of the ceremony. I longed to run away. If I could make it back to my bed and pull the covers over my head, I knew I would be safe, but I couldn't move an inch.

The twitching and squirming had stopped and I now found myself frozen like a statue at the center of the altar. My breath hitched and my throat felt choked, blocking any words from tumbling out of me. My eyes darted around, but now even the lone candle had been blown out.

I couldn't move, I couldn't talk, and I had no control. I was suffocating in the darkness. This was going to be the end for me. I just knew it.

In my peripheral vision, I saw a shadow creep forward through the darkness. Even though, I couldn't see. I knew that it was Martha slinking up to me knife in hand.

My instincts were correct as I soon heard Martha's voice from the seeming abyss. At least, it was a form of Martha's voice. The tone I heard was lower than Martha's usual pitch. The strange words she spoke were graveled and grated against my sensitive ears.

As Martha droned on a small voice crept unbidden into the back of my mind. It was a voice that I was now becoming familiar with. It was the deep, purring voice from that day at the shop and at the storm class. It was the sound of the creature that haunted me and now it's words bounced around my skull like an echo in a cave.

Fool, it sighed, *to think that these silly superstitions may drive away me. Why their fear and anger only make me stronger. Makes us stronger.*

I could feel Martha's hot breath on my face. A cloud past over the trees and I sliver of moonlight shone down making the knife Martha held glimmer. The very knife that I know saw was dangling right above my heart.

She's going to kill me. She's going to kill me and there is nothing that I can do about it.

The only part of my body that I had any control over was my eyes. I clamped them shut and waiting for the strike to impale my chest.

But the blow never came.

There came a high shriek and clamor followed by a the sound of a blunt thud. I gasped as my breath returned to me. I rolled over to my side clutching my throat, shivering as my blood rapidly cooled.

I was grabbed roughly by my shoulders and was tossed onto the ground. I wheezed and pried open my eyes, when new arms wrapped around me and started to half drag me across the grass.

"Run," It was Mai's voice as she tugged me forward. I stumbled and trailed after her only glancing once behind me.

A scuffle had broken out at the Sanctuary. Shadows wrestled on the ground. I couldn't make out one blur from the next, but I recognized Tamara's battle cry bellowing through the night. A slight figure, that I figured for Elaina was darting amongst them tripping and scratching as she passed.

Mai tugged on my arm, nearly popping it out of the socket. We sprinted through the trees and underbrush until we met the edge of the clearing. As the sun started to creep over the horizon, I collapsed to my knees, wheezing to catch my breath.

Mai hoisted me up and forced me to keep running. We raced over the GinWhiskey Bridge my lungs burning with every step. Finally, I couldn't take it anymore and I pulled Mai backwards and dragged her to a small alley between two store fronts.

"Where are we going," I gasped, "What's happening?"

"I don't know," Mai sighed, "I don't know where we're going, but I knew we had to get you away from there."

"How did you know where I was?" I questioned.

"You never came up to bed. When we went down to the common room you weren't there. At first, we thought you were taking a walk or something, but then Aria came down. She told us that Martha talked to you earlier. She kept urging us to go to the Sanctuary, but she wouldn't tell us why. We got worried about you and left. When we got there and saw the ceremony that they were performing on you, we knew that we had to stop them or they were going to kill you."

So, they really were going to stab me. I was right. Bile rose up and a I keeled over to the side of the alley, my sick splashed against the wall and the toe of my shoes. When I was finished, I slide my back against the wall until I was sitting with my head between my knees.

"They told me they were going to help me," I cried, "What were they really trying to do to me?"

"It's an old ceremony. I don't think it's been performed in America for years," Mai explained, "It's an extreme form of exorcism. Most these rituals are a simple cleansing of the spirit and mind and are harmless. But what they were doing was to expel an extremely dark force. It banishes the evil spirit from this word but," Mai looks at me warily, "Whoever is hosting the spirit cannot survive."

"Oh my God," I whisper, "What am I going to do? What's wrong with me?"

"Mirah," Mai slides down next me against wall, "What is going on with you. I want to do what I can to help you, but you have to tell me a bit more about what's going on. Why did they want to perform that ritual on you?

Mai, Elania, and Tamara had been so good to me. I knew the least I could do was tell them the truth. So, there against the cool, rough wall, I told Mai everything about the events that led to last night.

When I had finished, we sat in silence for a long time just lost in our thoughts. Then with sharp nod to herself, Mai leapt up and offered her hand to me.

"This is going to end. We are going to get you help that does not involve you dead on top of some dirty slab in the middle of the woods. I'll figure out a plan. I always do."

I grabbed Mai's hand and she pulled me up from the ground. I wrapped me arms around her in gratitude.

"I don't deserve you guys. I don't know how I will ever be able to thank you."

"Well don't thank me yet," Mai responded, "We need to find someplace to hide out for a while. We have done damage to our bindings to the coven. They will be looking for us soon and who knows what will happen if they find us. Hopefully, then I can get word to Tamara and Elaina and they can meet us there if they're Okay."

Mai's face darkened with worry. I thought about bringing Mai to my aunt's house, but I'm sure that would be the first place the coven would go to look for me. There was only one place I could think of that we could go where they would not think to look for us. It was also the only place I thought of that would even bother to welcome us. I hated to endanger anyone, but there was no other choice. With newfound determination, I grabbed Mai by the wrist and started to lead her out of the alley.

"I know where to go."

Chapter Eighteen:

Darien

It had been hours since Jude and I had begun this game of wits. But, through careful planning, I was sure that I would be able to smite my enemy for good.

"Full house," Jude announced dryly.

"Seriously!" I yelled, "No one ever beats me at cards!"

"Well it looks like I have. Nine times. Would you like to make it ten?"

"Bring it demon boy,"

I had begun shuffling the cards when there was a thunderous knock on the theater door. I looked at Jude in confusion, until he motioned me to open the door.

I crept the door open carefully, wary as to who would be waiting on the other side. I was stunned to find that it was Mirah looking pale and bedraggled leaning against a striking Asian girl. Without a word, the two of them charged into the theater and collapsed in a heap onto the nearest seat.

"Um, come on in," I said jokingly. They both looked absolutely exhausted and judging by their torn and dirt clothes, they had traveled a long way to get here.

"Would you ladies like something to drink?" I asked trying to be polite despite the circumstances.

"Water. Please," They answered in unison. I scurried to the backstage kitchen to get them something to drink.

Backstage, Jude was waiting for me with his arms crossed sternly over his chest.

"Who is it?" He questioned me.

"Mirah and some girl I've never met before," I answered honestly. I was so startled I didn't even know what else to say to Jude.

"They just showed up," I continued, "and they both look like they have seen better days."

"This is perfect," Jude clapped once, "Now we've got her right where we want her and she'll have no choice but to trust you now."

Yeah, super sweet," I responded sarcastically, "but what am I supposed to do about the other girl. I don't even know who she is."

"I'll come up with you and take care of the other girl," Jude answered confidently, "You just focus on getting that little witch to sign the master's book."

I nodded and Jude bounded away to the front lobby of the theater. I didn't want to say anything to Jude, but I found that with each passing day, the deal I had made seemed less appealing to me.

I liked Mirah as a person. She was pretty yes, but from what I have seen of her, she seems like a genuinely nice person and I still had no idea what was going to happen to her if I got her to sign their dark book. I couldn't stop thinking about what kind of life I could be forcing Mirah into. I didn't know it was worth it.

I didn't have much time to think as Jude's snippy yell beckoned for me. I grabbed two bottles of water and made my way back to where the girls were.

When I returned, I handed them both a bottle of water which they drank greedily as Jude and I stared at each other bewildered.

"I take it you girls were a little thirsty," I joked trying to break the tension.

"Very," Mirah gasped taking a breath from gulping her water, "Thank you so much."

"Well, what's going on?" I asked, "You girls on the run."

"It's a long story, but you're not totally wrong," Mirah sighs looking weary.

"Who are you?" The Asian girl asks brazenly. She stares directly into my eyes and I gulp, but charge on ahead with as much charm as I could muster.

"Darien Burron," I grin holding out my hand, but she doesn't take it. So, I awkwardly drop it back to my side.

"He's my friend," Mirah interrupts obviously trying to placate the tension in the room, "He's a magician and this is his theater that he very kindly has let us in."

"Mai Sato," The Asian girl snips to me with a curt jut of her head, "Thanks for your help," She adds somewhat sheepishly.

"I'm always happy to help Mirah," I respond trying to hide my annoyance with Mai's tone, "But can you ladies give me a bit more information about what's going on. I'm a bit in the dark right now, and if there are going to be thugs banging down my theater door, I'd like to have at least a little bit of warning."

The two girls stare at each other in a silent conversation. After a few moments, Mirah stands up and glides over to me.

"Darien, you have been such a huge help to me over the past few days and you deserve to know the truth,"

"Mirah," Mai warns, but Mirah continues on with a look of determination across her normally tranquil face.

"You should know that what I'm about to tell you is a lot and I understand if you don't believe what I'm about to tell you. It's going to sound crazy, but I swear to you that I'm telling the truth. I also want you to know that I understand if you don't want to see me again."

"You're not going to tell me something horrible like you've murdered someone or have a boyfriend, are you?"

She smiles slightly, "No. It's a bit more… unusual than all of that. Can we talk in private?" She thrusts her head towards Mai and gives a curious look to Jude who is twitching and pacing behind me.

"Of course, I answer, "Let's go talk in my office. My… new business partner will keep Mai company while I'm gone, won't you Jude?"

Jude and Mai eyeball each other carefully, Jude's nose wiggled with discomfort, but he settled down in the now open seat beside Mai.

Satisfied, I led Mirah to one of the back offices of the theater. It was the cleanest of the offices and very spacious. It used to be Gerald's main room of operation, but since the theater had been forcefully taken over by new management, it had become my own personal lair.

When we entered, I first sat at the large, oak desk chair with a wheeled office chair. However, this felt far to formal, like I was performing some sort of interview. Instead, I opted to sit on the large oak desk itself, while Mirah sat neatly on a small, black, leather couch.

"This is all a very long story," Mirah warned.

"I've got all day," I answered crossing my ankle over my knee and leaning my head in my hands to display my interest.

Mirah took a deep breath and then the sage started pouring out of her. She must have talked for at least a good hour, but I was so stunned and enraptured with what she was saying, it felt like no time at all.

When she had finished, she let out a long sigh and then looked at me with nervous anticipation.

I was stunned. The part of her story that worried me the most, was that I knew what was possessing her. I knew who crept into her mind and whispered dark pleas into her ear. It had to be the Dark Lord. There could be no other option. I didn't know what to say. If I told her the truth it could destroy her and end up ruining my own cause. But to not tell her seemed wrong. She had been so open and honest with me, to not try and help her seemed like an ultimate betrayal.

The whole reason you were even brought back to life was to betray her you idiot. A nasty voice whispered in the back of my mind. I cracked my knuckles and flexed my fingers. It was true. There was no point in getting more involved then I had to. There was no outcoming of this relationship ending well.

I forced a smile back on my face and grabbed Mirah's hands in mine.

"This is a lot to take in," I choked out, "but there is something about you Mirah, something about you that I just can't explain."

I got down on to bended knee which may have been a bit over dramatic, but I really wanted to play up the knight in shining armor vibe I was going for.

"I need you to know that I believe you, and that I promise to do whatever I can to help you. Please. Feel free to stay as long as you need."

Mirah grimaced at my vow. Okay, I deserved that. I was definitely laying it on a bit thick.

But I watched as she corrected her expression to a serene smile, and she held my hands tighter.

"Thank you so much," She replied softly, "I can't tell you how much I appreciate all this. I promise we won't bother you for long and we won't just laze around the theater. If you need help cleaning, or setting up the show…"

"It really is my pleasure I promise," I assured her, "But since your open to it, I'll offer my proposition from earlier again. I need a female assistant. Someone pretty to distract the audience while I set up the tricks. Jude is a charming as a rock, but you'd be perfect for the job."

"Deal," Mirah answered curtly. Desperation shone through her eyes, she needed me and I had her exactly where I needed her.

"Besides," Mirah added quickly, "This could turn out to be kind of fun." She gave me a small hug and darted back to the front of the theater.

I wanted to call after her, but my chest was burning too much from her embrace for me to do more than double over.

Yes. It was for certain. There was no way this story was going to end well.

CHAPTER NINETEEN:

MIRAH

It was hit with a wave of relief. I knew Mai and I were not out of the clear yet, but at least we had some place to stay. I halted and looked back at Darien who was watching me with an expression that I could not read.

We hadn't known each other long, but I already I owed him more than I could ever pay back. I kept waiting for another shoe to drop. He would demand something from me that would send me running out the door, or that he would finally have enough of me and show me the door, but nothing I said or did seem to bother him.

There must be something terribly wrong with him, I decided. No one could truly be that nice. I was sure that I find his true colors eventually, but for now, I had bigger issues to deal with and at least Mai and I could deal with them with a roof over our heads.

I made my way back to the front of theater. Mai and Jude seemed to be locked in a battle of wits questioning one another.

"Your parents? What about them? What do they do?" Mai asked with a smirk.

"Oh, my father does fatherly work and my mother does motherly work. You?" Jude returned with a similar cunning smile.

"The opposite. My father does the motherly work and my mother does the fatherly work," Mai quipped.

"How progressive," Jude drawled.

"Quite. Now, since you work at a magician's theater, I assume you know how to do a couple of tricks. What sort of magic do you know how to do?" Mai queried her eyes gleaming.

I coughed to get their attention. Startled, the both looked at me, though I noticed that they were still eyeing each other suspiciously from the corner of their eyes.

"Sorry to interrupt," I muttered, "Mai can I talk to you in private for a moment?"

Mai gave a nod to Jude who returned it with a small bow and she followed me outside the theater.

"Darien said we can stay here as long as we need," I sighed.

"What's the catch," Mai asked not missing a beat.

"We just need to help getting everything ready for the show. Darien needs a stage assistant and you could probably help out with tickets or something."

"Oh, I'm sure he needs and "assistant," Mai retorted rolling her eyes.

"It's not like that," spluttered swatting her away, "Besides, we need someplace to stay and helping out around the theater is the least we can do."

"I don't trust these people Mirah," Mai warns scanning around her, "There's something off about both of those guys. No one ever offers this much without wanting something in return."

"I get your thinking, but we really don't have any other options right now. This is the best we've got."

Mai let out a loud huff, but started stomping her way back into the theater.

"I'll help," Mai added, "But if anyone tries to shove me in some sort of death box, there is going to be a fight."

"I think that's my job," I laughed,

Mai turned around to say something in response, but I saw her eyes look towards the sky and her face grew pale. I peered back to where she was looking and felt my blood go cold. The sky was rapidly growing dark as storm clouds inched away from the direction of the forest towards town. In the distance, you could hear the rumble of thunder and crackles of lighting.

Mai and I stared at each other panicked. This was ordinary storm. This was a storm of magic coming right towards us. We were safe for now, but the storm was coming closer every minute. We needed a plan and we need one quick.

* * *

Over the next couple of days, Mai and I tried to busy ourselves with work at the theater, to keep our minds off the ever-growing storm cloud making its way towards us. Darien and I practiced various routines until we had them down with a military-like precision and with each day, our trust in one another grew. I had to trust that he would not actually saw me in half and he had to trust that I would be able to follow direction and position myself correctly as to not get stabbed. During practice we laughed a lot, and I found myself growing more and more comfortable at the theater and knew, in the back of my mind, that it had nothing to do with the stuffy setting around me.

As Darien and I worked, Jude scurried around the theater organizing everything from animal cage to fake flowers all while constantly dusting.

Mai stomped around the neighborhood strong arming people into buying tickets for the show all while keeping one ear to the ground for any word of strange people or occurrences spreading through the town.

Thankfully, there seemed to be no word of any odd events other than the dark storms clouds that ever lingered over the area. We didn't know what the coven was planning, but it seemed for now, our location was still unknown.

Mai tried to get ahold of Elaina and Tamara through various incantations and technologies, but we hadn't heard a peep from either of them. Mai kept insisting that they were probably fine, or that they were hiding out somewhere until it was safer for them to contact us, but with each day her excuses became thinner and I could tell that she was getting worried.

For over a week we all worked together, slowly becoming more comfortable with one another prepping during the day and then spending long nights in the back rooms of the theater telling stories and getting brutally beaten in cards by Jude. I wanted so desperately to relax and embrace this weird new family that we had become, but with every darkening day, I knew that this piece could not last forever.

We all knew it. Jude paced fervently back and forth, Mai was constantly casting her eyes to the sky, and I would catch Darien's burying his face in his hands when he thought no one was looking. No, this happiness would not last, but with unspoken determination we threw all our energy into the opening night of the show.

Before we knew it, it was finally time for the opening night. Mai had managed lure most of the members of the town to buy tickets for the event, so it looked like we were going to have a strong opening night.

The night before the show I sat in front of a vanity mirror and adjust the waves in my hair that Mai had recommended for me. My life had gone from rather ordinary to bizarre so quickly and I saw no end to it in sight. Mai and I still didn't have a plan on how to deal with the coven or how to get rid of whatever evil was inside me. I was lost on a path that I saw no end to, and I had the sinking feeling that I was going to end up trapped in the underbrush.

There was a light knock on the door, and Darien peeked his head in and gave me one of his thrilling smiles.

"Nervous?" He asked.

"A bit," I admitted. I was nervous, not for the show, but for the unseen future beyond the performance.

Oh, that's alright. It's perfectly normal to get the jitters before a show. But don't worry," He added wrapping his arms around me in gentle hug, "You are going to be amazing. The audience is going to eat it up." He pulled away but kept his hands gripped around my shoulders.

"You just have to trust me, Okay?" Darien looked into my eyes and I felt an electric current pass between our touch.

"I trust you," I swore and I found that I meant every word of it.

"Good," Darien whispered, his eyes softening. He gave me a swift kiss on the cheek. Then abruptly, he erected himself and adjusted the sleeves of his shirt. I could my face flush with surprise more than embarrassment. He glanced up at the clock on the wall and gave my shoulder a single shake.

"Well my dear Mirah, it looks like it's show time."

CHAPTER TWENTY:

DARIEN

I could hear the rumble of the crowd as they started to make their way to their seats. With the money we made tonight, even if the show was a complete flop, we should have made enough to at least get by for a few more weeks.

I peered through the crack in the curtain and watched as Mirah glided through the audience offering palm readings as they waited for the show to start. It was a gimmick we thought of to get people excited for the show and everyone seemed to be eating it up.

I sighed and pressed my back against the wall, fiddling with the cuffs of my sleeves. This was ridiculous. I should have just picked the money we needed and not bothered with this dog and pony show. I considered calling the whole thing off. Striding out onto the stage and telling everyone there has been a mistake and that they should just head on home

It would be easier to just scrap the show. That's it. The decision had been made. I pushed my shoulders back and started to make my way from behind the curtain, when I heard a sudden round of applause. I peered over to see Mirah smiling brightly, surrounded by an excited group of patrons.

I couldn't do it. We had all worked so hard and Mirah seemed so proud of her work. I couldn't throw it all away in the last minute. I pinched myself for even being so cowardly. I was Darien Burron, never in my life had I ever been a coward before.

I heard Mai close the doors to the theater, signaling that the show was going to begin soon and that people should start to take their seats. I made my way to my side of the stage. I looked across the stage to Mirah who had hustled herself to stage right. I gave her a wink for confidence which she returned with a nervous smile.

I motioned to Jude to dim the lights, but after he flipped the switches, I saw him stiffen. He scanned around him and his nose twitched like a hare smelling the air. I wanted to ask him what was wrong, but there was no time. It was my time for the spotlight.

* * *

The show went smoothly. The audience laughed at the jokes and gasped when they needed to. Jude did not miss a beat with the tech work, despite his harried demeanor, and Mirah was the perfect magician's assistant. She had a natural grace which enraptured the audience keeping their gaze away from my sleight of hand and she was able to contort herself easily into various props and boxes.

The final act was a classic maneuver that had been done countless times, but was still always a crowd pleaser. The trick involved Mirah laying down into a large box. I closed the box, throw a sheet over it, tapped it around and mumbled some random incantations. Then, I would wave a saw in the air, cut through the box, and then pull the two halves of the bow away to show two halves of Mirah's body. I would then connect the boxes back together, give it another spin and put Mirah back together again

To the audience, it looked like I had magically sawed Mirah in half, when in reality there are two boxes. One shows the head and the other shows the feet. In reality the feet are

117

artificial, and Mirah is able to curl her legs up in the other box, so that the saw never touches her.

Everything was going according to plan. Mirah was positioned correctly in the box and I had "sawed" through the two boxes and separated them to the amusement of the crowd.

However, as I was about to put the pieces back together, there was a rush of static charge in the air and the power went out.

The crowd muttered and rustled around, confused as to whether this was part of the show or not. I staggered around in the dark, trying to think of an excuse to give the audience, when as suddenly as they went out, the lights returned.

I let out a great exhale of relief and was just about to make a joke to the audience to clear the mood, when the audience broke out in applause. Amused, at the audience's enthusiasm for light I turned to Mirah to give a laugh, but when I looked at the box, my stomach dropped.

The boxes had been placed back together, but Mirah had disappeared. Instead, a white rabbit sat still upon the top of the box. My heart raced as I gave a nervous bow to the applause. Hurriedly, I thanked them for coming to the show and raced backstage to tell Jude to close the curtain.

Backstage, Jude was nowhere to be found. I pulled the curtain closed and and frantically tried to piece together what had happened, when a small voice squeaked up at me from down by my feet.

"We need to leave immediately. It's not safe here anymore and we need to get Mirah before those hags do."

I looked down to see the white rabbit from the box looking up at me, wiggling its nose impatiently.

"Jude?" I blurted out flabbergasted.

"Those witches from Mirah's coven were here. The slunk backstage and before I knew it they turned me into this. Joke's on them though, I've had to live in worse forms than this."

I grabbed Jude by the ears gently so that I could hear him more clearly, "What happened to Mirah? What about Mai?"

"They took Mirah when the power went out. It all happened so fast, I didn't have a chance to warn you. I haven't been to the front of the theater yet, so I don't know what happened to Mai."

I rushed to the front lobby, bobbing my head politely to the remaining patrons who wanted to comment on the show and pet Jude whom I carried under the crook of my arm. I managed to elbow my way to the ticket booth and my heart dropped.

Mai was gone. Money and papers were scattered on the ticket booth floor and smoking burn marks gave signs to a scuffle.

"They got Mai," I whispered to Jude disheartened. I ducked down under the desk in the booth and held Jude aloft.

"What are we going to do?" I asked bewildered.

"We need to get Mirah to sign that book before those witches kill her," Jude squealed frantically, "Or all of this would have been for nothing!"

I knew I needed to complete my deal or I was going to end up some demon worm wiggling around the underworld for the rest of eternity. But even I had to admit to myself, that I wanted to save Mirah more reasons than that. With new found resolution I jumped up, swinging a protesting Jude around in the air.

"I know where we need to go."

* * *

Over the past few days, Mirah and Mai had made mention of their coven in the forest. I knew that's where the witches must have taken them. I wasn't sure exactly in the woods they would be, but I'm sure if I moved quickly, I would be able to stumble upon it. I mean, how hidden can a whole school full of witches be?

I had run out of the theater, not even bothering to lock it behind me. I hailed a cab and shoved Jude into my jacket. The forest, itself was not difficult to find and I was able to make it to the edge of the forest in record time. It was traipsing my way through the woods that turned out to be the real challenge.

In his new form, Jude was able to hop his way nimbly through the underbrush, but I kept tripping over roots and smacking into the branches. The path was winding and much of it was covered in ferns and other plant life, so it didn't take me long to find myself hopelessly lost.

With each passing minute, I found myself starting to panic more and more. I could feel myself getting further and further away from Mirah, but I had no idea what to do. At one point I slipped on the same pile of wet leaves that I had earlier and realized that we were going in circles.

"It's over Jude," I declared, throwing my arms in the air as the dampness from the foliage started to creep its way into my pants, "I don't know if were even going to be able to get out of this place let alone find Mirah. I'm half tempted to just try and torch the whole thing down and work from there."

"We're close. I can feel the magic," Jude insisted, "I just can't make way of these paths."

"That's one of Martha's spells," A bored voice called out from the high branches of the trees.

Darien and Jude looked up to see a sharp-faced African American girl clamber down easily from a nearby tree.

"It's a confusion spell meant to protect the coven from outsiders. Only a witch is able to find the Sanctuary. Anyone else becomes lost in the forest until they decide to leave or die."

"Who are you," Jude and I blurted out in unison.

"You have a talking rabbit. That's fun," She answered dryly, "My name is Ariea. I have the feeling you're looking for Mirah and I guess you're going to need my help."

She started to walk away. Jude and I looked at each other in confusion, unsure if we should follow this strange girl.

"Well hurry up," She called to us, not bothering to look back.

With an unspoken agreement Jude and I ran after her down the dark, gnarled path.

It was luck that we had Ariea as a guide. Ariea and I stayed to the edge of the path as Jude hopped along in the woods. Ariea had just made the motioned that we were closing in on our destination when a small squeak grabbed our attention.

Jude had slipped into a dark cravat hidden in the ground. It was covered in leaves and roots making it almost impossible to seen by the human eye.

"What the…" I stammered rushing towards Jude.

"Don't move," Ariea hissed as she leaned over the hole, "The more you wiggle the further you dig yourself into the ground."

She reached in and carefully lifted a dirty Jude out of the trap, "These were created long ago to ensnare trespassers and for hunting. The more you struggle the more stuck you become until you eventually are too far down in the ground to get out."

"The trick," Ariea continued as she brushed the filth off of Jude's fur, "Is if you fall down there to remain perfectly still. Then if your careful, you can quickly hoist yourself out, but you only have a couple tries before the hole starts to sink.

"Charming," Jude muttered shaking his head.

"Let's go," Ariea ordered and we followed her further into the woods, though Jude kept to the path this time.

It didn't take long for us to reach our destination. There was a beautiful clearing in the woods, surrounded by wildflowers. In the center was some sort of stone with carvings engrained on it.

Ariea motioned for us to creep down and stay silent, pointing towards two women. One wore a hood of green while the other wore a red cloak. They appeared to be guarding the premises.

"We're going to have to get past them in order to save Mirah and the others." Ariea explained.

"Marvelous. How do you suppose we accomplish that?" Jude squeaked with irritation.

"I'm glad you asked bunny boy," Ariea clipped, hoisting Jude into the air, "Because you're going to be our main distraction."

CHAPTER TWENTY-ONE: MIRAH

I blinked open my eyes and winced in pain. My head was pounding. I gently rubbed my head and I could feel a large lump on the base of my scalp. Behind me I could hear two voices chatting back and forth between on another.

"Well, it looks like we're all going to die together."

"I suppose so. Mirah might get a separate ceremony, but I think they're going to take the rest of us out in one go."

"I mean that's kind of nice. If I have to get murdered at least I get to be killed with my friends."

"Yeah and if we all die together that means that no one has to be sad when we're gone. It is sort of sweet."

I recognized those voices. I turned around to see Tamara and Elaina sitting on the floor casually as if they were enjoying a midsummer's picnic.

"Oh good! You're up," Tamara clapped.

"We were starting to get worried. How many fingers am I holding up," Elaina murmured holding up her fingers.

"Three," I mumbled drowsily, "Where are we?"

"Good. No concussion," Elaina noted.

"It appears that we are in some sort of underground dungeon," Tamara explained looking around, "I didn't even know this existed, but I guess you learn something new every day."

"How long have you guys been trapped here," I asked, forcing myself to sit up despite my aching head. I was seat on cold, hard earth. Tamara and Elaina were filthy with dirt and perspiration. Above us gnarled, thick roots curled around the ceiling. The walls were of gray rock chipped away by both time and man. There were no windows, only a single, black stone. On our side of the door there was no doorknob or lock. Only someone on the other side of the door would be able to open in, and even then, I wasn't sure how.

"It's hard to know for sure, Elaina whispered, "But it's been a while. We were put down here after that night in the woods."

"That was weeks ago!" I exclaim.

"Was it? Well then, I guess it's good that you and Mai joined us down here. As much as I love Elaina's company. It was starting to get a bit dull down here." Tamara said casually.

"How can you guys be so calm," I spluttered, bewildered by their blasé attitude at being caged and scheduled for death.

"Like I said," Tamara explained, "We've been down here for a while. Besides, you can't get anything done if you panic. If we're to escape, which I assume is what we all want. We need to keep our heads together and stay calm. Elaina's taught me that since we got locked down here."

"The first night, Tamara pounded on the wall so hard, she nearly broke her hand," Elaina added in her hushed tone.

Tamara looked at her still bruised hand and grimaced. Elaina gave Tamara a supportive rub of the shoulder and continued, "We've been trying to figure out how to get out of here, but there's more than locks to this place. There's old magic here that's beyond our skill. So, we've been stuck, but maybe now with you and when Mai wakes up, we'll be able to figure something out.

I turned to see Mai's figure slumped over in the corner. It was the most still I had ever seen her and it made me sick to my stomach.

"Is she okay?" I asked nervously.

"She's still alive," Tamara answered, "I think she got a bit more beat up than you though, so we'll have to see what kind of condition she is in when she wakes up."

My stomach turns as I swallow a scream. This is all my fault. These girls are trapped here because of me. Mai is seriously hurt because of me. They are going to die because of me.

"Let them kill me," I announce, "You guys have done more than enough for me. You don't deserve this. Let me try and make a deal with them. They can exorcise me and I won't give a fuss, but as long as they let you guys go unharmed. I'll take the blame. I'll tell them I made you do everything."

I felt tears well up in my eyes and start to stream down my cheeks. I had never been much of a crier, but since I moved out of my aunt's house I've been blubbering all over the place.

"Mirah don't be stupid," Tamara argued.

"No listen to me," I interrupted, "You guys have done so much for me. I can't keep letting you put yourselves out for me. I owe you guys so much. Please let me help you."

"For god's sake, you are such a drama queen," A muffled voice echoed out from the corner.

"Mai!" We all shouted in unison. Tamara and Elaina ran over to her. I tried to rush over, but I was hit with a wave of dizziness, so I stayed planted on the ground.

Mai weakly waved them aside, "Stop fussing. I'm fine. Their lucky that they got a jump on me or I would have smitten those bitches to the ground."

Tamara and Elaina laughed, but I could see the concern in their eyes. Despite her bravado, Mai was incredibly pale and bruised.

Groaning, Mai lifted a hand and pointed her index finger at me, "As for you missy, you're lucky that I can't get up right now, or I would go over there and kick your ass. We did not go through all of this trouble to save you the first time, for you to then just throw it all away by letting yourself get killed."

"Exactly," Tamara said firmly, "We're going to make a plan and we are going to get out of here."

"Even if we do get out of here, they will never stop looking me. They will never stop hunting us! You guys know that!" I argued passionately.

The cell was now quiet. Tamara and Elaina looked at each other with fresh concern. Finally, Mai's frail voice broke through the silence.

"She's right."

"Mai!" Tamara cried out in disgust, "We are not going to let Mirah die!"

"I didn't say that," Mai croaked, "But I am saying that Mirah has a strong point. Even if we do manage to get out of the cell and make a break for it, they'll be after us in less than twenty-four hours. I mean look what happened when we helped Mirah the first time. We can't spend our whole lives looking over our shoulders, and in the end, we'll never really be able to outrun them."

"Well, what do you suggest?" Elaina whispered so softly that I had to strain to hear her.

"We need to break the coven," Mai said i n a matter of fact tone, "If the binds that hold this coven together are broken, they will no longer have any sort of hold over us. We will be free to leave as we wish and we will no longer have to obey their rules. Also, we will no longer be traceable to them, or least, not as easily."

"These cells were made to hold witch hunters from long ago, or practitioners of the dark arts who wanted to infiltrate the coven. The spells that bind this coven come from some of the oldest magic known to man," Tamara sputtered, "How on Earth are we going to break those spells."

"Ladies, it's simple. My father was a lawyer and before he ditched my mom and I he taught me one important lesson: Before you sign a contract, always look for the loophole. So, you see, we just need to find the loophole."

"How are we supposed to do that when we're trapped down here?" I blurted out.

"Help me up," Mai announced holding her arms up into the air. Bewildered, Tamara stood over Mai and carefully helped her rise to her feet.

Mai grimaced and shook, but she managed to get onto her two feet. She swayed and held herself up against the wall catching her breath. After a deep exhale, Mai turned and threw us all a brilliant smile.

"Stand up. Perfect. Step one of my plan is completed. Now that the hard part's over, it's time to get out this rat hole. What's the plan ladies?"

Tamara and Elaina nodded with determination, "Funny you should ask Mai, because Elaina and I were thinking of a plan before you two woke up," Tamara explained, "It's going to take a little acting on your part though Mai."

"Well Mirah and I just spent out time on the run holed up in a magician's theater. Mirah's been getting all of the spotlight though. So, tell me ladies," Mai wheezed, "When's my cue."

Chapter Twenty-Two: Darien

Ariea and I watched Jude hop across the tall grass. It was adorable. I was never going to let Jude live this moment down. With ease, he bounced past the two guards who pointed with amusement at the unusual rabbit who dared to get so close to them.

Jude then bounded into the forest and the witches returned to their watch. What they didn't know what that Jude had crept up behind them and leapt with all of his little might onto a green hooded witch's back. She fell forward onto the ground, but I think that had to do more with the surprise of the force, rather than any sort of strength.

I lost it. I mean. I'm only human. The ridiculous sight of a rabbit taking that woman down and the strain on my nerves was too much for me. I doubled over laughing. Clamping my hand tightly over my mouth the restrain the noise as tears of laughter welled up in my eyes.

Aria rolled her eyes at me and pulled on my sleeve. "For God's sake, let's go."

Aria dragged me with her as she ran out from the cover and threw a cloud a violet smoke at the other witch. The red cloaked witch was so busy staring in bewilderment by the random hare attack that had appeared before her, she didn't even have time to respond.

The guard in red shrieked once in surprise, but after inhaling the smoke that Ariea sent forth, she quickly collapsed to the ground. As for the other witch, she was still stuck on the ground, as every time she tried to get up, Jude would hop up as hard as he could and bounce off of her head to keep her forced to the ground.

"Do we have to stop him?" I asked chuckling.

"Oh, grow up," Ariea scolded me. The more time I spent with Ariea, the more that I got the impression that she would not be very fun at parties.

Once we got closer, Ariea signaled for Jude to get off of the witch and she carefully blew the rest of her violet smoke into the guard's face. The witch went quiet and both guards laid peacefully still on the ground.

"Did you kill them?" Jude asked insistently.

"No. I just knocked them out for now. I hope it doesn't come to that, but if it does…" Ariea trailed off and shrugged, "Anyway, we'll worry about that when we have to. Right now, we need to find Mirah and the others."

Ariea slunk towards a clearing in the forest and Jude and I followed suit. We jogged as quickly and as quietly over branches and foliage until we reached what had to be the heart of the Sanctuary.

It was stunning. Brilliant tree houses twisted and twirled around towering Oak trees. The windows gleamed in the fading dusk and the fragrant smell of roses and lilac danced through the air.

I was so taken in by the beauty of this establishment, that I lost track of my surroundings. I tripped over a hidden vine and crashed into Ariea who was leading the path ahead of me.

"Get off me you idiot," Ariea hissed.

"Will you two shut up before we get caught and some godforsaken hag turns me into stew." Jude squeaked at us, his nose twitching int irritation.

I was about to tell him that there wasn't enough meat on him for any sort of satisfying meal and that he shouldn't give himself so much credit, when something blunt slammed into my right side and toppled on top of Ariea and I.

The added mass, along with the ache in my ribs, knocked the wind out of me. I laid gasping on the ground until a pair of surprisingly strong hands lifted me onto my feet.

"Who the hell are you?" A husky voice cried out in confusion.

"Darien. Ally to Mirah and Mai. You?"

"Tamara. Same," The stout girl replied.

"We were just coming to save you guys," Ariea wheezed, "How on Earth did you get free?"

"We'll explain as we get out of here, but we've got to move," A petite brunette whispered while glancing frantically over her shoulder, "Their going to be searching for us any second now, and Mai and Mirah are not exactly in the best condition for running."

Mirah.

I turned to see her leaning against a nearby tree gasping for air. She was incredibly pale and bruises marked the side of her face and arms. I called out to her. Tamara, shushed me immediately, but Mirah gave me an exhausted half-hearted wave of acknowledgement.

Mai was leaning against Ariea for support and she looked in even worse shape than Mirah. There was a sheen of sweet across her face and a large gash in her forehead still dripped with blood, forcing her to close one of her eyes. Her entire body was shaking and I feared that she would soon collapse.

"What are we waiting for!" Jude exclaimed jumping into the air impatiently, "Let's get out of here!"

"Jude?" Mai and Mirah whispered incredulously together.

"Did that rabbit just talk?" Tamara asked, "That's awesome!"

"We'll explain as we walk too," Jude answered, "but we need to move! Now!"

We hurried back as fast as we could. Tamara and Ariea each wrapped an arm around Mai and half dragged her through the forest. The petite brunette who introduced herself to me and Elaina helped me get Mirah onto my back. Mai and Mirah were safer this way, but the added weight was slowing all of us down.

"What about guards at the clearing?" Elaina panted.

"We took care of them," Ariea answered and explained how we managed to use Jude as a distraction to take down the guards.

"What are you doing out here?" Elaina inquired to Ariea.

"That night I knew that something wrong was going on. I snuck out to the forest and saw you all fighting. When they brought you to the dungeon, I didn't know how to help you. I slipped away, waiting for Mai or someone to come along and help me."

"Didn't anyone notice you were gone?" Elaine continued.

"No," Ariea answered curtly, "No one ever notices when I leave."

We marched in a solemn silence for a minute until Ariea turned to Tamara, "Now that you know what happened with us, you have to tell me how on Earth you got away," Ariea insisted.

"It wasn't easy," Tamara grunted as she hoisted Mai to a more comfortable position around her shoulders, "We were placed underneath the roots of the Sanctuary which is protected by multiple forms of magic and the only way to get in and out of the cell could only be accessed by someone outside of the cell. But Elaina and I had a lot of time to think and plan while we were trapped down there."

"We realized that the only way we were going to get out was if we could convince someone to open the door for us," Elaina added.

"But so far, we had barely interaction with anyone outside of the cell. Food appeared through a slot underneath the door that was too small and move too quickly for us to do anything about it. So, the only option we could think of was if they thought one of us was ill and they had to come in and check on us," Tamara explained.

"It wasn't a perfect plan," Elaina insisted. She picked up Jude to comfort herself, petting him gently on the head. I could tell that he wasn't happy about the situation, but he made no attempts to stop her affections either, "We couldn't know for sure if they would even bother to help us if one of us was sick. There was a good chance they would just leave us there to rot," Elaina remarked bitterly in her soft tone.

"But we had to try. We knew that we couldn't use Mirah. I mean they want her dead anyway, no offense," Tamara added to Mirah apologetically, "But, as you can see, it would be easy to convince anyone that Mai is incredibly ill and needs medical attention."

"I'm just a really good actress is all," Mai slurred as we dragged her on.

"Mhmm," Tamara sniffed, "Anyway, when our food appeared, we call out as loud as we could that Mai was sick and needed help. We begged for a long time, but finally, the coven healer opened the door followed by a guard. The guard made us line up against the wall with our hands up as she checked Mai. When the healer got really close…"

"Mai bolted up and grabbed her. It was quite impressive actually," Elaina finished.

"While Mai was fighting the healer, the rest of us took down the guard," Mirah interjected as she bounced on my back, "It was a difficult fight."

"Mai and Mirah were already hurt, so they ended up taking on even more damage," Tamara explained, "But we managed to knock them both out and get away."

"They're going to find out we're missing soon," Mai wheezed as we started to reach the end of the forest, "Once they do they will never stop hunting us, especially Mirah."

I clenched my jaw and hoisted Mirah further up on my back, "Well then, we'll just have to stay one step ahead of them," I called to Mai trying to sound casual.

Sunlight broke out bright amongst the tree. With a last heave of strength, we rushed out of the forest as fast as we could.

I stumbled giddily into the clearing. Plotting our next steps. The theater was a lost cause, but we could travel. Fly as far away from here as we could and start new lives. Mirah and I could forget about the darkness that chased us both for a while. I turned to Tamara to tell her that I had a plan, that we should make our way to the nearest bus station, when I saw her stop dead in her tracks. Elaina's eyes widened and I heard Mirah curse in my ear.

I looked ahead and saw a statuesque woman with red, curling hair standing before us. She was dressed entirely in black. On either side, she was flanked by women of various ages and sizes all in the similar dark attire.

"I suppose that tall drink of water and her minions are not a welcoming committee," I whispered to Mirah.

"That's Martha," Mirah whispered back, her voice trembling, "She's the head of our coven."

"So, this means…" I trailed off.

"It means we're royally screwed."

Chapter Twenty-Three: Mirah

This is it. This is the end. I thought. Martha and half of the coven was blocking us from escape. There was no way that we could get past them without any kind of fight, and even if Mai and I were in any sort of fighting shape, there were a lot more of them then there were of us.

"Ladies," Martha began holding her arms out as a gesture of peace, "Where do you think you're going?"

We all stood silently trying to think of our next plan of action. I couldn't bear it anymore. I had endangered so many people at this point. I could have people get into any more trouble because of me. I couldn't keep running.

I slid off of Darien's back and staggered towards Mirah with my hands held up.

"Mirah, what do you think you're doing," Darien hissed at me, but I ignored him and moved forward.

"You can have me!" I called out, "Just leave my friends alone! They don't deserve to be caged or hurt."

Martha's face softened, "It never had to come to this Mirah. We're a coven," She motioned towards the girls on either side of her, "We're here to help you."

"You were going to kill her!" Mai screamed even though her knees buckled with exhaustion.

There were a few mutters of concern from the members of the coven, but with the sweep of her hand, Martha silenced them, "It was never our intent to kill Mirah. We were trying to rid her of the darkness that dwells inside of her. It is a danger a coven to Mirah and the coven itself. True, the ceremony we were performing is dangerous. There is the chance for loss of life, but that can be said for almost any serious ritual a witch performs. But, we wanted to do everything we can to save Mirah. We still do."

"We know you're going to do the ceremony again!" Tamara shrieked.

"It is the only option we have of truly giving Mirah peace," Martha explained. Her face sag and for the first time she no longer looked regal, but sad and tired. Lines creased across her brow and her lips became saggy and weary.

"I will agree to this ceremony and I will give you no fight!" I yelled back to her, ignoring the protests behind me, "But you have to swear to me that my friends will be free and unharmed."

"Of course," Martha sighed, "You girls are still bound to this coven. We never want to have to lose a witch."

"Your cronies didn't exactly seem concerned about our welfare when they slapped Mirah and I around and threw us all down in some dungeon!" Mai protested.

"You make a valid point Mai, and I'm sorry that it had to come to this. However, you fought back violently yourself, so my girls had to do what they had to do."

"Can you promise me?!" I yelled. I didn't care anymore what would happen to me. I just needed to make sure that my friends would be safe.

"I promise you," Martha swore, "As long as you girls are bound to this coven, you will always be wanted here. We want to treat you with the utmost respect, but of course for safety reasons," Martha threw a side eye over at Mai, "We need the same respect from you."

"What about Darien?" I asked my heart pounding.

"The boy? He will be released. Of course, we will attempt to wipe his memory of our Sanctuary, but he will be left unharmed."

My heart sinks at the idea of Darien forgetting me, but I know it's for his best interest so I agree.

There are protests behind me as members of the coven move to grab our arms. Darien writhes and struggles, so much that it takes five witches to hold him down.

"Mirah you don't have to do this!" Darien screams, "I know another way!"

I try to ignore him as he was drug away from the edge of the forest. Jude and Ariea seemed to have slunk away before we were caught and were nowhere in sight. Those crafty snakes.

"Mirah you're being a coward!" Mai shrieks as they drag her away.

You promised me you wouldn't hurt them!" I call to Martha in panic.

"I won't. They will not be harmed in any way. That I swear to you. But they have not promised that they will not bring harm to me or other members of this coven. The state they seem to be in now, gives me cause to worry, so until they calm down and they can be trusted, they will be put into rooms where they cannot attack any of us or themselves."

I shiver as I watch Darien and my friends being torn away from me in separate directions. I knew that it's for the best. I can't keep endangering the people I care about on my behalf.

Martha strides up to me holds out her hands. I wonder if she is going to strike me, but to my surprise, she wraps her arms around me in an awkward embrace.

"We're going to take care of all of this Mirah. But it won't be easy," She holds me at arm's length and assesses me up and down.

"Am I going to die?" I ask trying to keep the fear out of my voice.

"Honestly," Matha sighs, "You might. But," She tightens the grip around my shoulders, "You seem to be a strong girl Mirah. I believe you can get through this."

I give her a forced smile and Martha dismisses the other members of the coven back into the forest.

"We finish this tonight Mirah," Martha announces her eyes growing dark, "This time there will be no interruptions. Do you understand?"

I return Martha's gaze and give her a single nod. Then she wraps her arms around my shoulders and leads me back into the dark mystery of the trees.

Chapter Twenty-Four: Darien

Man, either these witches are lifting weights between potions class or I need to work out more because these girls were kicking my ass.

I was tossed on my butt in a secluded part of the nearby field under a weeping willow tree. A benevolent looking, gray haired woman glided up to me. She looked if your grandmother went through a goth phase in high school and never really got over it.

"I'm sorry you had to get involved with this my dear," She began as she hovered over me, "But I promise you, that this won't hurt a bit and you'll be back to normal in no time."

She began to lower her hand to my forehead. Now, I would never condone hurting an elderly woman, or anyone for that matter, but desperate times call for desperate actions.

I leaned back on my hands and delivered a swift kick to the woman's knee. She gave a loud grunt of pain and bent over to grab the injured area. I took this quick distraction to haul myself up and sprint back into the forest.

I could hear the two witches who originally dragged me away chasing after me.

"You fool!" I heard the old woman calling behind, "If you're not caught first, you'll be lost in an instant!"

Ah crap, she's got me there. Well right now being lost in the woods seemed better than being tackled by these magical linebackers and having my memory snatched. Hurriedly, I sped on, back into the clearing. The girls behind my cried-out taunts and curses, but I was to focused on not losing my footing to bother to look behind me.

I had to lose them. I racked my brain for tricks until a desperate idea popped into my mind.

I hide tailed it off the path into the forest clearing. I skidded on some wet leaves and went sliding across the ground. As I laid there panting, I felt my hand lightly give way to the ground underneath it. I had found what I needed.

"Alakazam!" I bellowed for some flair as I dove into the murky ground. The earth was cold and slimy and I had to bite down on my cheek to keep myself from wriggling about.

Thankfully, I didn't dive too deep into the ground. There was only a thin layer of dirt between me and the surface. I could feel the soil around me tremble as the witches rang by. I could hear their angry grunts as the continued to search for me.

When I was sure that the cost was clear, I inhaled deeply and, with as much force as I could muster, clawed my way out of the ground. I could feel the force of the ground trying to pull me back down, this little trap was not happy that its prey escaped. But I managed to wrap my hands around a large rock embedded in the ground and I hoisted myself heaving onto the dewy grass.

I crept as fast I could after the witches, hoping that they would lead me back to the Sanctuary. I followed their wheezes and curses as they ran. I had to admit I had no idea what I would do when I got to the Sanctuary, but at least I would be closer to Mirah.

I followed the girls until the trees began to clear. What to do? What to do? I continued charging forward. Just keep running. I thought. Running seems to be working for me right now. Now with blind determination, I began to sprint hoping that I would stumble onto a solution.

Then, like magic, I really did stumble onto a solution. Literally. I crashed into it. In my wild rush, I barreled into an unsuspecting figure and we both rolled clumsily across the grass.

Groaning, I was shoved off the figure and smacked onto the ground. Then before I could even get my surroundings, I was grabbed by the scuff of my neck and dragged behind a large Oak tree.

"How do you manage to keep running into me," hissed Ariea.

"I'm just lucky I guess," I snarked still smarting from the ache around my neck, "How did you get away?"

I'm a shadow witch," Ariea explained with a small puff of pride, "It's a very rare witch type. I can use my magic to appear as nothing more than a shadow for a short period of time. It's very useful in sticky situations you see. So, when I saw Martha, I knew that there was no way we were all going to get away, so I slipped into my shadow form and slunk into the shade of the trees to try and make a plan."

"What is your plan?" I asked impressed.

"Well…" Ariea trailed off losing some of her bravado, "I haven't really decided yet. If I were smart, I would have escaped when I got the chance, but…"

"We've got to help the others,"

"Unfortunately," Ariea sighs and grabs my arm dragging me away. We make our way to the clearing from before. The sun is starting to set over the horizon and I can hear the chants of a strange tongue growing louder and louder with each step.

"We may be too late," Ariea notes stone faced.

I open my mouth to argue with her, but I'm cut off by a shrill scream piercing the evening air.

CHAPTER TWENTY-FIVE: MIRAH

Martha was apparently tired of waiting around to try and murder me. After the others had been taken away. She brought me immediately to the Sanctuary even though it was still light out.

She urged me to lay on the altar and, even though she was trying to keep her voice calm, there was a sharpness to her commands and her eyes were darting frantically every which way.

The only other woman, besides Martha, was the fragile clairvoyant I recognized from the meeting with Martha in her office ages ago. She was holding a black candle and whispering softly to herself.

The altar was cool to the touch. The pain and tension I was feeling was exhausting. I was tired of running. I was tired of trying to fight. I just wanted to sleep.

I wasn't even scared anymore. I just wanted my friends to be safe. I laid my head down against the slab. Martha peered over me and softly brushed the hair out of my face. The gesture was almost motherly. I thought of the mother that I never knew. There was still so much about myself and the world that I didn't know.

Martha nodded towards the clairvoyant. She handed her the curved dagger and lit the black candle with the flick of her hand.

"You're going to be alright Mirah. We're going to take care of you," Martha whispered. I could tell from the sorrow in her eyes that I there was no chance this was going to end happily.

I swallowed the tears that welled in my eyes and nodded to Mirah. In unison, Martha and the clairvoyant began to speak in an unknown language. I could the fire in my blood and the beads of sweat start to form in the middle of my forehead. There was a rushing in my ears and the tips of my fingers started to tingle.

The witches grew louder. I felt myself grow hotter and hotter. My breathing began to itch and I was unable to control the increasing convulsions that began wracking my body.

As I gasped for air, over the cool tones of the chanting came a low, dark voice. The voice in my head that clung to me no matter how hard I tried to shake it away.

Your stronger than them Mirah. That's what they are afraid of. Their scared that you will overthrow them.

I want to ignore the dark tone. But I was too tired, too weak and that cool voice was soothing to the heat that poured from my body. *Fight them Mirah.* It purred. *Stop trying to deny your own power.*

The tingle in my hand started to become sparks. Waves of energy pulsed through my body in even larger waves than the lighting class. It was too much. The heat. The energy. The droning from Martha's chants filled my ears. I couldn't breathe. I couldn't think. I was going to explode.

Even though my eyes were closed, I knew that Martha had come closer to me. I sense her presence hovering over me. Every sense was too heightened, even with the chanting, I could hear the dagger slicing through the air. Ready to plunge within me.

Martha's incants had now turned into bellows. Her screams pierced the forest sky. My convulsions grew larger. I no longer had any control over my body or thoughts, I was lost, except for the soft, low voice in my head that whispered a single command.

Unleash it.

I couldn't fight myself anymore. I finally allowed myself to let go. I shrieked as loud as I could and with every ounce of energy I had left. With each gasping breath, I felt the energy and fire that had been burning my insides pour out. It drained from my fingertips and out my mouth.

It was intoxicating. The chanting had now turned into screams. My howls mixed with the others. I didn't know why they were yelling, but I couldn't open my eyes to see. Intermingled with the wails of women, was a thunder of a laugh from deep in the crevices of my mind. Darkness curled around the corners of my thoughts and I was going to lose myself to that laugh when one sharp voiced slashed through the commotion inside of me.

"Mirah! No! Stop!"

Darien. I gritted my teeth and clawed my hand to the edge of the altar. With a savage grunt, I heaved myself over the edge of the slab and collapsed onto the earth.

The world around me suddenly became quiet. I clamped my eyes tight, but unbidden tears still managed to roll down my cheeks as I dug my nails into the soft dirt, deeply inhaling the smell of pure earth.

A firm hand grazed my trembling shoulders. "Mirah. My god, are you alright?"

I tried to nod, but sobs choked out of me. I clung to the ground. I didn't want to open my eyes. I didn't want to see the damage I had done.

"Mirah, please. I'm here. Please look at me." Darien whispered.

With enormous effort, I opened my eyes for the first time in what felt like years. I saw the grass beneath me, and with a heavy heart, turned around to face Darien and my own destruction.

Darien's face was dirty and his eyes looked tired. He tried to lift me up, but I dug myself further into the ground.

"What did I do?" I croaked. My voice was hoarse and my throat felt like it had been slashed with small knives.

"You didn't do anything," Darien began.

"Don't lie to me," I wept, "Tell me. I need to know."

There was a beat of silence, until a bored voice simply said, "You killed them."

I pushed myself up, ignoring Darien's reassurances. My eyes locked onto Ariea's honest, dark eyes. She lifted her eyebrows into a facial shrug and motioned with her head for me to look behind me.

Slowly, I turned to face the carnage that I had created. I saw two limp forms thrown haphazardly to the ground. I broke away from Darien and crawled my way to the nearest figure.

It was the clairvoyant. The remains of her slight figure and a few strands of her white hair were her only identifiers. Her flesh had been scarred and seared away. Her tiny bones were broken and twisted into unnatural contortions like a marionette thrown to the ground.

Everything was shattered. Her nose was broken. Her lips appeared to be torn away. The most horrifying part though, was that she no longer had any eyes. They had been burned into her head, so only ash filled sockets stared back at me.

I turned and vomited onto the ground horrified. I had killed people. I had become the monster that I always feared myself to be.

Cool hands held back my hair as I continued to regurgitate.

"Let it out." It was Ariea. Other than a few strokes to my hair, she was a statue. Waiting patiently for my next move.

When there was nothing more left in me. I laid on the ground and stared up into the sky. The sun had set and stars were starting to sprinkle their way across the night sky. The outline of a waxing moon shone down in a patient glow.

"Martha..." I asked, even though I already knew the answer.

"The same," Ariea answered simply.

"I really am a monster," I sighed defeated.

"I don't know what you are, but we can't stay here any longer," Ariea informed me, "People are going to come looking for Martha and when they discover this scene, things are not going to end well."

"Let them come," I croaked, "They'll hunt me down eventually anyway."

"Maybe not," Ariea said cryptically. She reached out a hand to pull me up and even though I tried my best, I didn't have the strength to rise to my fight.

"I've got it," Darien announced and slung me over his shoulder. I was too tired to fight and I knew I wouldn't be able to walk even if I wanted to.

We raced through the forest. In the position I was in, the only thing I could see was the grass rushing beneath me. It was dark, much darker than I had seen before. I forced myself to lift up my head. There were no more orbs. There was no light of any form to be seen.

We made a slow stop and Darien lowered me carefully onto the ground outside of the Main Hall.

"What happened to the lights?" I asked nervously.

"It's what I thought," Ariea answered, "The bind has been broken."

"The bind?" Darien inquired.

"It's a spell that connects each member of the coven to one another. Martha was the connector to all of the bindings. Without the connector, there is nothing to keep us together."

"What does that mean?" I asked.

"It means they won't be able to track you. It means we're independent from the coven," Ariea explained looking thoughtful.

"That's great!" Darien exclaimed, "What are we doing then? Let's get out of here."

"We're not leaving without Mai and the others," I insisted, "I'm not abandoning them."

Darien kicked his feet in frustration, "We don't even know where they are! We need to go! We can try and help them later when you're healed Mirah."

"I'm not going." I retorted.

"You're not exactly in a position to fight me. I will carry you out of here if I have to!" Darien exclaimed.

"I swear I'll bite you," I snarl.

Darien opens his mouth to argue, but Ariea puts her hands on both of our mouths.

"Shut up," She states bluntly, "Mirah, you are useless right now. You're going to just slow us down. Darien, get her out of here. I will find the others and meet up with you later."

"How will you know how to find us," I protest.

"I'll find a way. I always do," Ariea stated matter of factly.

Before I could argue, Darien swept me up. He mumbled something to Ariea that I couldn't hear and began jogging away from the Main Hall. I craned my neck to look back at Ariea. She didn't wave or call out. She just watched us with a solemn expression. Then in a blink of an eye, she was gone. It was like she just slipped away.

CHAPTER TWENTY-SIX:

DARIEN

I ran. I had no idea where I was going to go or what I was going to do. I just knew that I had to get out of these horrible woods and away from the madness that laid behind us.

I was afraid that I would get lost, but luckily, it seemed that my feet knew on instinct which way to go. After a while, I started to see the trees begin to thin and the outline of the edge of the forest. I shifted a squirming Mirah over my shoulder and continued to barrel onward.

When I saw the familiar clearing outside of the forest, I collapsed onto the ground to catch my breath. Mirah landed with a grunt on the ground and I wheezed and spat onto the wet grass. There was a sudden rustle in the tall grass beneath us. Without thinking, I grabbed a rock that laid beside me and threw it towards the grass.

I must have missed, because a small but powerful force ploughed into my chest making my crumble to the ground. I hacked trying to recapture the wind that had been knocked out of me. When I was able to refocus my eyes, I zeroed in on a small, pink triangle and then expanded my gaze to white fuzz surrounding dark, burning eyes.

"Jude? Where have you been?" I muttered bewildered.

"Bouncing around. I'm not an idiot. I know when to leave, unlike you morons. Speaking of which, you need to get up. Now. You're not safe yet," Jude squealed at me.

I grabbed Jude by the ears and placed him aside. I rolled over to my side and hoisted myself onto my feet. Then one thought flashed through my head. Mirah. I swung my head frantically back and forth, until I saw her half sitting, half leaning against a tree that she had managed to crawl too.

I stumbled my way towards her and then knelt carefully beside her. Her face was pale and sickly. Dirt clung to her fingernails and her clothes were filthy.

"I need to do something," Mirah croaked looking up at me with glazed eyes.

"Mirah…" I began, but Mirah interrupted me in a trembling voice.

"It's all my fault," Mirah cried, "Everything is all my fault. I hurt people. I hurt people and I am useless to stop it."

"Mirah," I whispered, "None of this is your fault."

"I killed people!" She screamed. There was nothing I could say. I didn't know how to comfort her.

"What can I do?" I begged, "I want to help you Mirah, I really do. But I don't want to watch you destroy yourself. You can't even walk right now. If I take you back there, I'm afraid that might be the end of you."

"It would be what I deserve." She whispered, looking up at me with cold eyes.

A chorus of screams suddenly echoed through the night sky. Mirah and I looked towards the dark abyss of the threes. Jude began hopping back and forth frantically, "We need to go!" Jude squeaked.

"No!" Mirah screamed, "I won't leave them! I need to make sure they are okay. They wouldn't leave me!" She began clawing at the tree trunk, trying to get herself onto her feet.

"Mirah! Stop!" I bellowed, "There is nothing you can do right now. You're just going to make things worse!"

"You asked me what you could do," Mirah snarled, "Help me up." She held out her hand, her blue eyes piercing into me making my chest start to burn.

"Even if we help you up, what exactly is your plan Mirah?" Jude's tiny squeak cried out.

"I'll figure it out as I go," Mirah retorted, not taking her desperate eyes off of me.

"Darien, please." She begged. Cries and screeching rose up again making my teeth grate.

I grabbed her hand and felt a surge of power. It was like experiencing the strongest electric shock that you could imagine.

"Darien, it's time," Jude hissed to me.

There was a pulsing in my chest. No not now. It's not right. She's weak. I can't do this right now. I don't think I can do this ever. The pulsing in my chest became a tugging, like someone was pulling on a heavy, tight string in my chest.

"Darien, what's wrong?" Mirah questioned, "What's going on?"

"What if there was a way you could save your friends?" Jude insisted, "What if you could not only get your strength back, but more powerful than ever before?"

"Jude. Stop," The pressure in my chest was suffocating, bringing me to my knees.

"What's going on?" Mirah screamed in concern.

Jude hops closer to me, "This is what you were brought back to do," Jude whispers fervently to me, "The master has decided that now is the time. Do. Your. Job."

The force behind my lungs was moving forward. It was tearing through my muscles, splitting apart me skin. I screamed and writhed on the ground without control. My body did not belong to me anymore. I could feel spit and foam slipping out of the corners of my mouth. My eyes rolled wildly, but I could catch glimpses of Mirah looking at me with an expression of pure horror.

"There is a book," Jude called to Mirah, "It resides inside of Darien. Sign it Mirah. Sign it and you can save your friends, you can help Darien, and you can have more power than you could ever have dreamed."

"What the hell kind of book is it? Who does it really belong too?" Mirah cried.

"I think you know," Jude answered solemnly.

The pain was excruciating. I wanted to hold the book in. I wanted time to think. I wanted time for Mirah to think. I wanted to be in control of the situation, but there was no use. This book was going to burst its way out of me and there was nothing I could do to stop it. I tried calling out to Mirah, but I couldn't form the words. Instead, all that came out was a garbled cry of agony.

"Why does he want me," Mirah whispered defeated, "What does the Dark Warlock want from me?"

I had to admit that I had chewed over this question myself. In the weeks that Mirah and I were preparing for the show. Why did the Darkness want Mirah so badly?

"I'm afraid I don't know," Jude replied, "It has never been my job ask questions. I just take my instructions and follow my orders."

"How long have you known this?" Mirah asked, frantically looking back and forth from Jude to me, "How long have you been working for him? Has this all been a trap?"

The book made an outline against the outside of my chest. I fell to the ground and cried out. It pushed on and on, until it clawed its way out of my body, leaving me gasping and bleeding.

Mirah stared at me wide eyed, but Jude pressed on with urgency, "Mirah, this is no trap. This is a lifeline. This is how you can be who you were meant to be. This can be the answers to all the questions. You can save everyone. You can understand who you are. Please Mirah. Darien is hurt, your friends may be getting tortured. Sign it."

The edges of my vision started to blur in a familiar manner. I knew this feeling. I was dying. Damn. It was a lot easier the first time.

"What's going to happen to me if I do sign?" Mirah whispered.

"I don't know," Jude answered truthfully, "But it's the only way."

Mirah gave a shaky nod and dug her nails into the ground, crawling towards me. I wanted to call out to her. I wanted to tell her that it wasn't worth it. She didn't know what she was getting herself into. I wanted to tell her that dying really wasn't so bad and that it was alright for her to let me go. But my throat felt torn to shreds from screaming and all I could manage was a gurgle of blood.

Jude watched, frozen in place, and Mirah inched her way closer to the book. I stretched my fingers out to try and snatch the book away, but I couldn't reach.

Finally, wrapped her hands around the book. As she stroked the spine of the book, I could feel the ground beneath me tremble and the air grow colder by degrees.

She tucked the book under her arm and used it as a kind of pick to drag herself to me. I wheezed and choked, praying that somehow, she would be able to read my mind and would know not to sign the book.

Mirah leaned over me. Strands of her hair tickled my face as she wiped away the stain of blood from my chin. She took a deep breath and kissed my forehead. Then turned to aim those piercing eyes at Jude. I was fading, the world around me going was going quiet, but I managed to hear Mirah call out to Jude in a crystal-clear voice.

"Where do I sign?"

CHAPTER TWENTY-SEVEN: MIRAH

It called to me. I wanted to help my friends. I was desperate to save Darien. But, on top of all of that, there was no denying the siren's song that sang to me from those ash be speckled pages.

I needed to find out what I am. I need to know what to do so that I don't hurt people anymore. Something was telling me that I may have just found my answer.

I grasped the spine of the book and felt a wave of warmth wash over me, like I had just submerged myself into a hot bath. With trembling hands, I flipped through the pages, words and names from endless languages flashed past me in a blur. My body was humming and my hands worked on instinct, as if they have always known where they needed to go.

Finally, I turned to a pure blank page. There was nothing written on it, but I knew deep in my gut that this was meant for me. I turned to Jude with a newfound determination.

"How am I supposed to sign this thing?"

Jude hopped around frantically trying to find some form of a writing utensil. But it wasn't like there was a pen lying in the middle of the grass. Jude looked at me with exasperated eyes and I turned to Darien. Any sign of color had been drained out of his face. His lips were stained with blood and his eyes were glazing over with each passing second. I was losing Darien right before my eyes and I had no idea what my friends were going through, I had to do something.

Desperately, I scoured the ground until I found a rock that look like it had sharp enough edges. I gritted my teeth and sliced the rough edge of the rock against my finger as hard as I could. Jude watched me as a hiss of pain slipped through my teeth. He gave me a last nod of approval and I dangled my bleeding index finger over the page. There was a roaring in my ears and behind the roar was a deep, low laugh reverberating in my head.

I was just about to place my finger on the page when I heard Darien call out to me in a low gurgle. I saw him reach his hand out to me and I grabbed it. He brushed my hand aside and tucked his hand behind my ear.

"You've got something behind your ear. Did you know that?" Darien choked.

I giggled sadly, "Oh yeah. What's that?"

He traced a line along my chin quietly. Then in an instant he shoved me aside and dove on to the book.

"What the…?!" I screamed as I turned and watched Darien take his bloodied hand and smear his name across the parchment.

"Darien! You've ruined everything!" Jude yelled.

The book began to vibrate in Darien's hands. A blinding, red-hot light poured outwards forcing me to turn away and cover my eyes. I couldn't see. A high-pitched screech arose and I clutched my ears, curling into a ball.

In that moment, I was blind, deaf, and in agonizing pain. My blood felt too hot for my body. My skin felt like to was covered in millions of tiny pins. I don't know if I screamed or cried, I just know that I wanted the pain to end.

Then as suddenly as it began, it ended. My seizing body relaxed. I could ear. When I blinked open my eyes, the light was gone and I could see the dark earth beneath me.

Darien. Gasping, I turned around. The book was gone. Darien was gone. There was no sign of either every existing.

"Darien," I whispered, feeling the panic grow inside if me.

"Darien!" I screamed crawling forward.

"He's gone Mirah," Jude called to me.

Gone where?!" I cried, "What the hell is going on?!"

I was exhausted, scared, and confused. I had never imagined that my life would end up with me begging a talking rabbit for answers.

"Please Jude," I whispered, "Tell me the truth."

Jude rose onto his hind legs. His small, pink nose wiggling into the night air, "I suppose there is no point in keeping anything from you now. What will happen, will happen at this point."

Jude proceed to then tell me everything. The deal Darien made with the Dark Warlock, the fact that Darien had died before, the fact that Jude himself has died before. It was a lot to take in.

I listened agape, as Jude finished his story. Soon my shock was replaced with a churning in my stomach. It was all a set up. I had placed my faith in them, my friend's faith in them, and in the end, they were planning to betray me.

"What does the Dark Warlock want we me?" I hissed between my teeth.

Jude opened his mouth to speak when a stream of bright, blue light streaked into the sky from the center of the forest. My friends. They were the only ones who were there for me without an ulterior motive.

I shot Jude a glare, and grabbed a nearby tree branch. With every ounce of upper body strength, I pulled myself up to my feet. Sweat poured down my face as I snapped the branch off the tree and limped my way back into the forest. Whether Jude followed me I didn't know and I didn't care. I just keep moving forward. One step after another, I made my way closer to that shining light.

At last, I stumbled past the Sanctuary. The bright light was growing brighter and I could start to hear the voices of the coven. I traipsed forward on instinct, until I made my way to the front of the Main Hall. The doors were wide open and the light sprang forth from within.

I staggered up the steps past the statues of the goddess. I could hear the clamor of voices from within the dining hall. Without thinking, I reached out to open the heavy doors to when I felt a hand grab me by the back of my collar and pull me backwards.

"What do you think you're doing?" Ariea hissed in my ear, "Are you trying to get yourself killed?"

"I need to help my friends," I whispered back surprised. There had been no sign of Ariea even being near me. It was like see appeared out of thin air.

"I told you I would handle it," Ariea snipped with annoyance, "You're just getting in my way."

"I saw the light and I thought you might need help," I insisted, "What's happening anyway."

"Their deciding on a new Martha," Ariea explained, "They need a new Coven head. Every second without one the coven is left unprotected and the binds are broken. Normally, before a Coven Head dies, she assigns one in her will. However," Ariea gave me an arch of her eyebrow, "Due to Martha's sudden death, they need to figure out who the Head is going to me on their own and let's just say that there is a lot of competition for the position."

'How do they decide?" I asked in wonder.

"It can be a difficult process. One that the previous Head overlooks over a period of time. It's not usually in one day." Ariea proves herself to be surprisingly strong as she continues to drag me silently towards the door.

"What is the process?" I ask as I struggle to free myself from her iron grasp.

"They must show that they are Proficient in all a areas of magic. It's something that can only be accomplished with years of training. Then the coven must make a vote on the contenders. The problem is all of the contenders keep voting for themselves, so there not getting anywhere."

"Where's Mai and the others?" I ask clawing into the air. I swear this girl must lift weights in her spare time.

"That's what I was working on before you interrupted me," Ariea snipped, "They're tied up in there. Once the new Head is decided on, there first order of duty is to hold trial for them."

"Trial?" I ask desperately.

"Yes. They need to decide what punishment they should receive for helping you. A couple softies say banishment, but most are saying death or torture and death."

I feel a surge of panic wash over me, "Let me go," I cry, "Let them kill me instead. I don't want people to suffer because of me anymore."

Ariea stops in her tracks and gives me a look that I cannot read. She calmly releases me and folds her arms across her chest.

"Go." Arieas says calmly.

"What," I replied bewildered.

"Listen, In the end, you need to do what's best for yourself in this world. You're nice and all, but you have proven to be a lot more trouble than what you are worth. So, if you want to go and sacrifice yourself, go ahead. I'm tired of trying to save you people. Anyway, having you dead might be for the best."

I balked her harsh words, but I knew that she was right. I had done my damage and now I have to try and mend things the best I can.

I gave Ariea a nod of thanks, which she returned with a shrug. With renewed energy, I marched my back to the dining room doors. I held my breath. My fate was inside that room. With a gulp, I turned the handle and charged into the room.

* * *

I looked up to see eyes of every color staring back at me. Some had expressions of fear, other of anger. One thing was for certain, no looked happy to see me.

Before, I could say a word, two women grabbed my arms and led me to the center of the room. In the middle was the gaping portal in which the shining, bright light sprung forth from.

"Cool light show," I joked with a tight smile as I tried to break the tension in the room.

"This ceremony is to determine a new Head of coven," a voice I recognized called out to me. I turned to see Kalani staring furiously back at me.

"This is for a ceremony that we wouldn't need to have if it wasn't for you," Kalani insisted, "You brought evil into this coven," She added, pointing towards my scarred hand for emphasis, "Then you kill our leader."

"What are you?" Some girl snarls from the back of the room.

"I don't know," I reply sadly, my eyes roaming the room until I lock eyes with Mai. Her, Tamara, and Elaina are tied by twisting branches to three chairs. Their mouths are gagged, but I can see the anger in Mai's eyes as they pierce into mine.

I tear my gaze away from Mai and turn to face the room, "I don't know what I am," I call out to the coven, "I don't know what I have done the things I have done. But I do know that I am sorry. I never meant for any of this to happen."

"You think sorry is enough!" Kalani shrieks and I shake my head.

"I know that no apology I make will ever be enough. But I stand before you all to make a final plea. Do with me as you wish. Kill me, torture me, turn me into a toad if you want to. But please, leave Mai, Tamara, and Elaina alone. They had nothing to do with what happened to Martha. They were only trying to be my friends. They shouldn't be punished for kindness."

There was a flurry of murmurs amongst the girls until Kalani help her hand up to silence them.

"You want a deal," Kalani croaked, "I'll give you a deal. I'll even let it up to the coven if they want to put it to a vote." Kalani turned and snapped her fingers at Mai, Tamara, and Elaina, "As of right now, we do not have a Head of coven. That means that there is nothing binding us together. I say we take this time and banish these three. You are to leave this coven, never to return. If you ever step foot in this forest again. It will be on pain of death. Understood?"

There was a general nodding of consensus amongst the witches, though I noticed a few of the more blood thirsty ones crossed their arms with frustration.

"As for you," Kalani continued, pointing her finger now at me, "The only fair sentence for you would be death."

Mai let out a muffled yell, but I nodded in agreement. The three of them were hoisted to their feet and brought roughly towards the door. Elaina's toes glided across the wooden floors as Mai and Tamara struggled against their captors, especially Tamara, who was giving her guards a very difficult time.

Kalani watched the struggle with disgust, until she shook her head and motioned for the witches holding me to bring me forward. I didn't fight. But I kept my head up as I strode towards my death.

"Kneel," Kalani commanded and I was forced down to my knees. Kalani held a glittering dagger before me, "I am going to make slit your throat and collect your blood. We can use it for spells," Kalani hissed, "At least your entire time here won't have been a total waste."

I wanted to spit in her face, but I didn't want to give her the satisfaction of seeing me angry. Instead, I stared forward willing myself to take deep breaths. I had never been one for prayers, but this seemed like the appropriate time to make one. The only issue was that I didn't know how. Instead, I tried to clear my mind the best I could. I closed my eyes and pictured a little white light moving slowly from the tips of my toes to the crown of my head, like I would do in yoga.

It was calming. The light spread through me and warmed my body, relaxing my muscles and easing my tension, the way a particularly good cup of tea works.

This isn't so bad I thought. I felt the cool chill of the blade press against my throat. I knew that Kalani was chanting something above me, but I ignored her. I pressed my eyes closer together and refocused back on that beautiful light.

It glided towards my throat. The heat counteracting the chill of the knife. I breathed deeply. Inhale. Exhale. Inhale. Exhale.

My throat grew hot. The light grew larger and brighter. It pulsed it's way outward until I heard Kalani give a high pitch yip and the dagger clattered to the ground.

I opened my eyes to see Kalani clutching a burnt hand, "What is wrong with you!" She screamed. I looked around and saw that the other girls had all taken a step back. The Mai, Tamara, Elaina, and their guards had stopped their scuffle to watch me with fascination. Many took a step back as if I were contagious.

Crap. I can't even die right. I raised my hands as a sign of peace. At the extension of my hand, every single light in the room extinguished. The light from the portal disappeared. The room became eerily quiet.

"He's here," Kalani whispered in horror, "Run girls!" Kalani yelled, "The Dar---,"

She didn't get to finish her sentence when a sharp wind whipped around the dining hall.

The Dark Warlock. He had finally come for me. Most of the members of the coven screamed and stampeded out of the door, desperate to escape. I didn't move. I was tired of running. It was time to finally get some answers.

From the depths of the portal in the ground emerged a tall, dark figure. I tried to get a good look at him, but his features kept morphing with the blink of an eye. One moment, he was a crooked, blind man hobbling his way towards me. The next second, he was a stunning Adonis with curling, blonde hair and eyes so blue that it actually hurt to look at them.

I was hypnotized watching his face twist from a snarling, animalistic sneer, to a serene middle-aged man. He was handsome, with dark hair greying at the temples and sides. He had a long, straight nose and a dark clipped beard. Even though, I had never seen him before, there was something terribly familiar about him.

With long strides, he approached me. Tamara cried out and tried to charge him, but with the flick of his wrist, Mai, Elaina, and Tamara were sent flying out the Dining Hall doors.

Kalani was muttering incantations behind me, but with a bemused smile he turned his hand and the words halted. Trembling, I turned to see that Kalani's mouth had been sealed and turned like the lock on a door. She groped at her mouth wide-eyed, until the Dark Warlock grabbed her by the throat and pulled her off the ground.

"Stop!" I cried, "Leave her alone."

"She was going to kill you," The Dark Warlock purred. I knew that voice. I knew that voice with all of my heart. It was the voice inside of my head. The voice that made me want to hurt people. He looked at me and unleashed a deep, low laugh that sent chills down my spine. I could no longer deny it. The Dark Warlock has always been inside of my head.

"What do you want?" I asked softly.

He turned Kalani's neck back and forth in his hand. Her face was changing from red to a dark shade of blue.

"Please. Put her down," I begged.

He lowered her down and released her throat. I saw a brief flash of relief in Kalani's eyes before the Dark Warlock snapped her neck with ease.

I screamed as I watched Kalani crumple to ground, "Why?! Why are you doing this?!"

"Mirah," He hissed, "She was trying to kill you. What kind of father would I be if I just stood by and let her get away with that?"

"Father?" I whispered in horror.

"I've been waiting a long-time for you my dear. I had to make sure that your power was strong enough, but I think your ready now. I think it's time that I finally brought you home."

"You're lying," I cried. This couldn't be real. It was impossible.

"I would never dream of lying to you," He replied brushing my cheek and making me shiver and sweat at the same time.

He chuckled, "I've been watching over you. You have your mother's looks that is for sure, but I see that you have my power."

All my life I had wondered who my father was. What kind of person he could be? It would be my luck that he would be the evilest person in the world. I didn't want to believe him, but as I looked into his cool, blue eyes that mirrored my own, I knew in my heart that he was telling the truth.

"I want to help you Mirah," He continued. His voice was like rich chocolate and I felt myself growing sleepy listening to him.

"You have so much power growing inside of you. You haven't even touched the surface. I wanted you to sign my book. That way you could come to me on your own accord, but unfortunately, I forgot that if you want anything important to get done in this world. You have to do it yourself."

"Darien," I muttered aloud.

"He's with me," The Dark Warlock replied, "Come with me Mirah. You can see him again. I can teach you how to perform magic beyond your wildest dreams. We could change the world together and you can finally understand who you are."

I was tempted. I was so terribly tempted. Before me was a creature offering me what I had always wanted: a father, a place to belong, a chance to not feel lost anymore. I could have cried.

I closed my eyes to keep the tears from spilling and in my mind, I could picture my aunts and my friends. I couldn't abandon them. Martha and Kalani dead because of me. I had wronged them. I couldn't go with him. I didn't want to hurt any more people.

"No." I responded coldly, "I am not like you and I never want to be like you."

As I spoke, I patted the ground blindly, until I wrapped my hand around the dagger that had fallen from Kalani's hand. It was still hot, but it didn't bother me as I lifted up the handle.

Now, leave and never come back!" I commanded lifting the knife towards his chest.

The Dark Warlock cocked his head, "Mirah, I'm disappointed. This is no way to talk to your father. Besides, do you really think you can get rid of me with a single knife. Don't be so naive."

"Leave!" I screamed.

He sighed and slapped me across the face, sending my sprawling to the ground. The knife flew out of my hand and skidded across the room into the shadows.

"Enough, Mirah. I am going to ask nicely one more time, or else I am going to have to bring you by force, which I really don't want to do. We are family after all."

He reached out his hand. I didn't know what to do. There was no weapon of any sort around me and I was far too weak to try and perform any kind of spell on him. So, I spat, right in the center of his palm,

"You disgusting little cur," He snarled as he shook the saliva out of his palm. In a blur he was suddenly tackled to the floor as Elaina, Mai, and Tamara bum rushed him to the floor.

"Get off my you little worms!" The Dark Wizard cried and with a wave of his arms all three girls were sent flying to a corner of the room. He raised and bashed their heads against the wall making them all cry out in pain.

I was too stunned to move, until I heard the quietest whisper in my ear, "Here,"

It was Ariea. She slipped the dagger back into the waistband of my pants and slunk back into the shadows before I could say another word.

I was frozen until I heard my father barking to me, "I said enough Mirah! Now come with me or I am going to keep bashing their little heads against the wall until their brains drip out of their noses."

I knew what I had to do. I walked towards him and nodded. He smirked and reached out his hand. I got near enough that I could smell the ash and smoke on his skin. It was like he embodied fire itself. I wrapped my arms around him in an embrace. He did not hold me in return, but rather was rooted to the ground in a second of shock.

That second was what I needed. As quickly, as I could I grabbed the knife from my side and then plunged it into his back. The Dark Lord let out an ear-piercing screech and I plunged the knife twice more into his back. He threw me away from him and stumbled backwards leaving a trail of dark blood.

The Dark Lord never took his eyes of me. He made his way to the edge of the portal and unleashed one final guttural laugh, "You really are like your father. You'll see that in the end Mirah." He lifted his hand palm forward into the air, where his blood once laid spilled immediately became bursts of fire leaping into the air. The Dark Lord winked at me, "I'll make sure to tell Darien you said hello." Then he toppled backwards into the depths of the portal.

I ran to the edge of the portal, but when I peered down, I saw nothing but an empty abyss.

"Mirah we have to get out of here!" Ariea screamed heaving one Tamara's arm over her shoulder and Mai grabbed the other. Elaina floated around nervously, and motioned for me to follow.

We raced out of the Main Hall coughing and gasping from the smoke. We rolled onto the grace and watched wordlessly as the Main Hall was engulfed by flames. The fire spread from tree to tree devouring everything in sight.

"What about the other girls?" I cried.

"There long gone," Elaina answered, "I can't hear their thoughts anymore. They are too far away."

"They were smart and ran off when they had the chance," Ariea sighed.

"We need to get out of here too. Mai announced. The coven is broken. It's not safe here anymore."

We sprinted as best we could out of the burning forest until we finally made our way to the open clearing. I looked up at the sky. It normally would have been a clear, night sky, but the smoke from the trees curled around the skyline covering any light. I saw the outline of rabbit ears in the distance. Jude. I tried to ignore him but he hopped up next to us desperately.

"What happened?" Jude squeaked.

"Where will we go?" Tamara asked nervously. Ignoring Jude's question.

"The theater?" I offered.

"No," Mai answered, "It's not safe. The coven found us once there. People will be able to find us again. We need to go underground. Somewhere completely off the grid."

"But, why?" Tamara sighed, "Can't we go home."

"Do you really think the Dark Warlock is dead. Do you think he will ever stop hunting Mirah?" Mai replied in a clipped tone.

"You guys don't-" I started, but Mai interrupted.

"No offense, but this isn't just about you. That guys wants to destroy everything that is good in this world, and I don't think he wants to just play catch with you and catch up. I think he needs you. We need to make sure that whatever he's planning never comes to fruition."

"We need a plan," Ariea stated simply, "We need to find a way to defeat him for good."

"Yes. I'm so glad there is a handy dandy how to on how to defeat the King of Darkness. I wish I had thought of that before." Mai snarked.

"There is no way to defeat him!" Jude insisted, "He's beyond any normal mortal."

Ariea opened her mouth to argue, but I held up my hand to stop her.

"I know where we need to go." I announced, "We can't stay long, but it's the only place we can find some answers."

"Where's that?" Ariea barked.

"My house. I need to know what really happened with my mother. Maybe if I can understand that, then we can figure out what to do next."

The girls looked at one another and shrugged in unison.

"And you sir," I added grabbing Jude by the ears, "Are coming with us. Along the way you are going to tell us every bit of information you know or we'll feed you to a hungry dog. Do you understand?"

Jude agreed even though he scrunched up his little nose in frustration.

"It's better than nothing," Tamara announced, "Are your aunts good cooks?"

"The best," I laughed half-heartedly. We made our way towards the twinkling lights of town and away from the destruction behind us. We couldn't look back, there was nothing left to save. The past had burned away. All we could do was look forward and hope we can protect the future.

CHAPTER TWENTY-EIGHT: DARIEN

You know, I thought I what to expect when it came to death after dying the first time. I just that just goes to show you should never assume. As Gerald always said, when you assume you make an ass out of…

The chains around my wrists and ankle dug tighter into my flesh making me grit my teeth in agony. I regret ever complaining about Purgatory. This was so much worse. The chains then relaxed and I felt myself gasp with relief.

I could hear the sound of heavy footsteps of rocky ground. I had a feeling that this relief was not going to last very long.

"Darien Burron," I low, deep voice called to me.

"Present," I answered with the sad lift of my finger.

"I must admit that I'm terribly disappointed. I had such high hopes for you, but you turned out to be a worse failure than I could have even imagined."

I looked up to see a monstrous man. All of the features were too exaggerated making the complete picture disturbing. The face was too long and ended at a sharp, pointed chin. The nose was upturned into slits and the lips were split into a hideous pointed smile that stretched across the entire face. The only thing that looked remotely normal was the eyes. They were a cool, blue looking at me with disdain.

"I'm sorry Mr. Dark Warlock Sir," I croaked, "I was never very good at following orders.

The chains burrowed themselves into my body. Tearing away at muscle and bone. I begged for forgiveness. I begged for the agony to end.

"Remember boy, you signed my book. I own you now. So, if I want to tear you skin of inch by inch and feed it to you. I can." The Dark Lord informed me calmly.

"I won't back talk again. I'm sorry!" I howled.

Finally, when he was satisfied, he loosened the chains. He slunk close to me and lifted my chin examining my face.

"You may have failed before, but there is still a chance that there may be some use for you." The Dark Lord muttered. He then let out a laugh that bounced through the walls. Then with a snap of his fingers, he tightened the chains and walked away. I called out to him for mercy, but the only response I got was,

"Yes boy, I will find a use for you. I just need to find the right time."

Other titles by BLKDOG Publishing which you may enjoy

Arthur: Shadow of a God
By Richard Denham

King Arthur has fascinated the Western world for over a thousand years and yet we still know nothing more about him now than we did then. Layer upon layer of heroics and exploits has been piled upon him to the point where history, legend and myth have become hopelessly entangled.

In recent years, there has been a sort of scholarly consensus that 'the once and future king' was clearly some sort of Romano-British warlord, heroically stemming the tide of wave after wave of Saxon invaders after the end of Roman rule. But surprisingly, and no matter how much we enjoy this narrative, there is actually next-to-nothing solid to support this theory except the wishful thinking of understandably bitter contemporaries. The sources and scholarship used to support the 'real Arthur' are as much tentative guesswork and pushing 'evidence' to the extreme to fit in with this version as anything involving magic swords, wizards and dragons. Even Archaeology remains silent. Arthur is, and always has been, the square peg that refuses to fit neatly into the historians round hole.

Arthur: Shadow of a God gives a fascinating overview of Britain's lost hero and casts a light over an often-overlooked and somewhat inconvenient truth; Arthur was almost certainly not a man at all, but a god. He is linked inextricably to the world of Celtic folklore and Druidic traditions. Whereas tyrants like Nero and Caligula were men who fancied themselves gods; is it not possible that Arthur was a god we have turned into a man? Perhaps then there is a truth here. Arthur, 'The King under the Mountain'; sleeping until his return will never return, after all, because he doesn't need to. Arthur the god never left in the first place and remains as popular today as he ever was. His legend echoes in stories, films and games that are every bit as imaginative and fanciful as that which the minds of talented bards such as Taliesin and Aneirin came up with when the mists of the 'dark ages' still swirled over Britain – and perhaps that is a good thing after all, most at home in the imaginations of children and adults alike – being the Arthur his believers want him to be.

Broken
(Book I of The Breach Chronicles)
By Ivy Logan

Half-blood sorceress, Talia, had a unique childhood. It might have been bereft of dolls but not of love. Instructed in combat skills and trained to escape detection, she was schooled to face an unknown menace. Yet, when her family's worst nightmare comes to pass, Talia finds her protected life spinning out of control. Everything she believes in, and everyone she loves, is cruelly snatched away. Talia is forced to flee the attentions of a mad king and denied her supernatural legacy.

She chooses the path of retribution, devoid of love and friendship, but learns that sometimes love is received even if not sought.

'Broken' is a tale about Talia's coming of age, reuniting with her family and seeking vengeance. Most of all it chronicles Talia's rise from the ashes and her journey into finding herself again.

Read Talia's epic saga of love, sacrifice, friendship, and discovering the hero within set against a background of time travel and supernatural forces.

Consumed
By Justin Alcala

Sergeant Nathaniel Brannick is trapped in Victorian London during a period of disease, crime, and insatiable vices. One night, Brannick returns from work to find an eerie messenger in his flat who warns him of dark things to come.

When his next case involves a victim who suffered from consumption, he uncovers clues that lead him to believe the messenger's warning. Despite his incredulity, he can't help but wonder if the practical man he once was has been altered by an investigation encompassed in the paranormal. That is, until he meets the witch hunters, and everything takes a turn for the worse.

Weirder War Two
By Richard Denham & Michael Jecks

Did a Warner Bros. cartoon prophesize the use of the atom bomb? Did the Allies really plan to use stink bombs on the enemy? Why did the Nazis make their own version of Titanic and why were polar bear photographs appearing throughout Europe?

The Second World War was the bloodiest of all wars. Mass armies of men trudged, flew or rode from battlefields as far away as North Africa to central Europe, from India to Burma, from the Philippines to the borders of Japan. It saw the first aircraft carrier sea battle, and the indiscriminate use of terror against civilian populations in ways not seen since the Thirty Years War. Nuclear and incendiary bombs erased entire cities. V weapons brought new horror from the skies: the V1 with their hideous grumbling engines, the V2 with sudden, unexpected death. People were systematically starved: in Britain food had to be rationed because of the stranglehold of U-Boats, while in Holland the German blockage of food and fuel saw 30,000 die of starvation in the winter of 1944/5. It was a catastrophe for millions.

At a time of such enormous crisis, scientists sought ever more inventive weapons, or devices to help halt the war.

Civilians were involved as never before, with women taking up new trades, proving themselves as capable as their male predecessors whether in the factories or the fields.

The stories in this book are of courage, of ingenuity, of hilarity in some cases, or of great sadness, but they are all thought-provoking - and rather weird. So whether you are interested in the last Polish cavalry charge, the Blackout Ripper, Dada, or Ghandi's attempt to stop the bloodshed, welcome to the Weirder War Two!

Click Bait
By Gillian Philip

A funny joke's a funny joke. Eddie Doolan doesn't think twice about adapting it to fit a tragic local news story and posting it on social media.

It's less of a joke when his drunken post goes viral. It stops being funny altogether when Eddie ends up jobless, friendless and ostracised by the whole town of Langburn. This isn't how he wanted to achieve fame.

Eddie knows he's blown his relationship with rich girl Lily Cumnock. It's Lily's possessive and controlling father Brodie who fires him from his job - and makes sure he won't find another decent one in Langburn. And Eddie doesn't even have Flo to fall back on - his old nan died some six months ago, and Eddie is still recovering from the death of the woman who raised him and who loved him unconditionally.

Under siege from the press, and facing charges not just for the joke but for a history of abusive behaviour on the internet, Eddie grows increasingly paranoid and desperate. The only people still speaking to him are Crow, a neglected kid who relies on Eddie for food and company, and Sid, the local gamekeeper's granddaughter. It's Sid who offers Eddie a refuge and an understanding ear.

But she also offers him an illegal shotgun - and as Eddie's life spirals downwards, and his efforts at redemption are thwarted at every turn, the gun starts to look like the answer to all his problems.

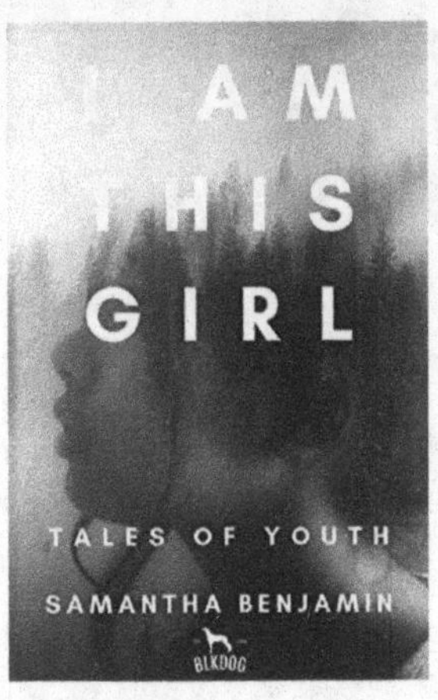

I Am This Girl: Tales of Youth
By Samantha Benjamin

I Am This Girl: Tales of Youth is a charming and moving story of a young woman's journey through the trials of tribulations of growing up. When Phil and Natalie first reveal that they want to move to Morpington, their daughter Tammy isn't thrilled - It's up North - Tammy hates up North. Her new life begins as a struggle, her new friendships at school are strained and she lives with the daily fear of bumping into her nemesis, Lorraine, in the corridors.

Though perhaps things aren't that bad after all. Tammy discovers up North isn't in fact as terrible as she feared and a fresh start may have been just what she needed. Somewhere no-one knows her and she can be whoever she wants to be.

www.ingramcontent.com/pod-product-compliance
Lightning Source LLC
Chambersburg PA
CBHW012015050726

47590CB00009B/3186